ALSO BY
PETER MATTHIESSEN

Fiction

Race Rock

Partisans

Raditzer

At Play in the Fields
of the Lord

Far Tortuga

Nonfiction

The Wind Birds

Under the Mountain Wall

The Cloud Forest

Wildlife in America

Sal Si Puedes

Blue Meridian

The Tree Where Man Was Born

The Snow Leopard

Sand Rivers

In the Spirit of Crazy Horse

Indian Country

Nine-Headed Dragon River

Men's Lives

ON THE RIVER STYX
AND OTHER STORIES

PETER MATTHIESSEN

VINTAGE BOOKS
A DIVISION OF RANDOM HOUSE, INC.
NEW YORK

FIRST VINTAGE BOOKS EDITION, JUNE 1990

Copyright 1951, 1953,
© 1957, 1958, 1963, 1978, 1985, 1988, 1989 by
Peter Matthiessen

"Sadie" and "The Fifth Day" were first
published in *The Atlantic*. "Late in the Season"
was first published in *New World Writing*
(NAL). "Travelin Man" was first published in
Harper's Magazine. "The Wolves of Aguila"
was first published in *Harper's Bazaar*. "Horse
Latitudes" was published by *Antaeus* (originally
published in *Venture* as "Horace and Hassid").
"Midnight Turning Gray" was first published in
The Saturday Evening Post. "On the River Styx"
was first published in *Esquire*. "Lumumba Lives"
was first published in *Wigwag*.

Most of the stories in this collection were
originally published in book form in *Midnight
Turning Gray*, published by Ampersand Press in 1984.

Library of Congress Cataloging-in-Publication Data
Matthiessen, Peter.
On the river Styx and other stories /
Peter Matthiessen.
p.   cm.
ISBN 0-679-72852-X
I. Title.
PS3563.A858405   1990   813'.54—dc 20
89-40508
CIP

FOR SHERRY

*My friend
for fifty years,
who pestered me to
return to fiction
before the smoke
clears*

AUTHOR'S NOTE

Some years ago I was very pleased when my editor at Random House suggested I put together a collection of short stories. I had scarcely written one since my first years as a writer, in the fifties, when I wrote close to thirty. Most of those early stories revealed very little besides the ambition of the new writer to try a variety of tones and voices—male and female, black and white, rich and poor, rural and urban—but perhaps a dozen had actually been published in one place or another, and among these I hoped to rediscover ten that might deserve a new life in a book. Finding but seven, I notified Random House that the new collection was not to be. (Subsequently, those seven stories were published by the Ampersand Press in Rhode Island in a small chapbook, under the title of the most recent, "Midnight Turning Gray," written in the early sixties.)

For two decades, no more stories were written. Instead I wrote novels and a bit too much nonfiction. In recent years, with a long novel under way, I kept my hand in with two new stories, considerably longer and more ambitious than the early ones. With another early story, now rewritten, they seemed to round out this collection.

The ten stories are arranged in chronological order, from "Sadie," sold to *The Atlantic* during my senior year in college (1950), to "Lumumba Lives," which appeared in the pilot issue of *Wigwag* (1988).

It's still fun to write short stories, I discover, and of course one hopes that in close to forty years there has been a little bit of progress.

Peter Matthiessen
Sagaponack, New York
December 1988

CONTENTS

ON THE RIVER STYX

AND OTHER STORIES

SADIE

I was over in Cady last February to see about their dogs, which they say is the best in Georgia. I was told to see this Mister Pentland, and if he weren't there, a feller name of Dewey Floyd.

That morning I come into the stable yard about half past eight, and they had the mules all ready, and two wagons rigged out. A couple of stable niggers was throwing dogs into the wagons. Over against the wall a man was leaning where the sun was, switching pebbles with a stick and talking to a big nigger boy with boots on. The nigger saw me coming and spoke to the man leaning on the wall. I said good morning when he looked up.

"Mornin," he said. He squinted out from under his hat. "You Mister Pentland?"

"Nope. Name's Floyd."

"Mine's Les Webster. I come about the dogs."

"Well, I'm pleased to know you, Mister Webster. We's fixin to run 'em now. Want to get out while the coveys is still feedin in the open." He nodded toward the wagons, which were pulling off down the road. The nigger nodded toward the wagons, too, but when I looked at him, he looked down, grinning, to slap the dust off his boots. You could see he hadn't had them boots too long.

Floyd was rolling a cigarette with his free hand. "Time we get you rigged out with a woods pony, you can foller us down that road. Mister Pentland is meetin me and the rigs over to Binny's Churchyard, and we're working out from there."

The nigger boy snickered at the way Floyd said "Mister" Pentland. Floyd looked at him a minute.

"This here's Buster," he said finally. "Buster'll get you a pony and take you out to Binny's. I reckon Mister Pentland's the one to see if you take a likin to any of the dawgs."

Dewey Floyd switched a stone with his stick, then pushed himself away from the wall like he was tired and walked slowly across the yard. He was tall and skinny, dressed in a white field jacket and soiled khakis which hung out over his knee boots. There was something funny about the way he moved, just like the way he talked—sort of soft and quiet and not really getting anyplace, and that stick switching back and forth, slow, like the tail on a cat.

Buster come out of the stable now with two horses. I climbed on and headed after Floyd, and Buster right behind me, hollering at the other niggers to get out of his way.

Now he was prancing all over that red clay road, grinning like a damn fool. "Mistuh Dewey say ah's to take you out to Binny's Hant-yard."

4

"I heard him."

"Yessuh."

Buster was making his horse prance by slapping the reins. He kept looking over at me to see if it was okay to talk. "Ah guess you-all ain' acquainted wid des heah hants out to Binny's?"

"Who told you there was ghosts there, Buster?"

"Mistuh Dewey Floyd. Mistuh Dewey, he live a long time in de swamp. He say dey ain' no foolin wid hants, an' ah don't truck wid 'em."

"Maybe he's ridin you."

"Whuffo' he wan' go foolin Bustuh? Ain' got no call to do dat."

Buster was staring at me, real uncertain. I didn't say nothing, just grinned.

"Now Mistuh Pentland, he say dey ain' none. He say Mistuh Dewey ain' no diff'rint den black folks. No hant gone fool wid a Yankee man, don' seem like."

I looked at him then, and he turned away like he'd said something wrong. "He your boss?"

"Yessuh."

"How about Mister Floyd?"

"Yessuh. Bofe 'em. Leastways, de Yankee man's de boss o' de outfit, an' ah kinda wuks fo' him, but mos'ly ah wuks wid Mistuh Dewey Floyd. It's him dat got me de job. Ah's de spottah. When a dawg is p'intin, ah hollers, an' when a dawg is los', ah fines him."

Buster was grinning again, and slapping the reins on the horse's neck. He stretched his legs out in the stirrups so's both of us could get a look at his boots. We rode along and didn't talk no more.

5

I SEEN THE DOGS FIRST, in the cornfield on the left past the churchyard, running in among the broken stalks. There was a black-and-white setter paired off with a little lemon pointer. The two wagon rigs were lying back on the road, a nigger driving each, and two men on horses were watching from the edge of the field. One of them was Dewey Floyd. The other headed over to me and the nigger.

Buster stopped whistling. "Heah he come," he whispered. He swung his horse wide and galloped for the wagons, the man yelling at him all the way.

Pentland turned his horse around and fell in beside me.

"You got a couple of nice-looking rigs there, Mister Pentland."

"Joe'll do fine. I guess first names are okay in the same business, huh?" Pentland laughed loudly, even for a big man. "What the hell," he said.

"Yeah," I said. He looked at me. "Name's Les," I said.

"Okay, Les. Yeah, the rigs are okay. Twelve dogs to a rig, two out at a time, and each rig's got a special dog for singles. The owner wants the best, and I guess I got it for him, all right. Les, you're gonna like these dogs. Just look at that Sadie bitch out there and tell me I ain't got a right to be proud."

Somebody had a right to be proud, for sure. The lemon pointer come out real pretty from behind a pile of stalks and swung into a tight point, and the setter right behind her.

"P'int!" hollers the nigger.

I watched Floyd.

"I guess you see how the setter dog's honoring her point," said Pentland. He laughed and spat on the ground.

Floyd was talking soft to the dogs: "Whoa-a-up, Sadie, eas-y, eas-y, whoa-a-up, Caesar, eas-y, boy, eas-y, eas-y . . ."

Then the quail got up, and the way he handled the gun I knew he wouldn't miss: he took a bird off each side of the covey rise, neat as anything, and then he was talking again. "Daid, Caesar, daid, day-ud bird, Sadie, eas-y, eas-y . . ."

"He's good with the dogs," I said. "Damn good."

"Hell, it's not him, it's the dogs." Pentland spat again, only a different way.

"Maybe, but they mind him good. And he's handy with that gun."

Pentland looked at me like I'd shot a dog by mistake. "He ain't been poaching twenty years for nothing! I ain't never seen the bastard miss a bird, but that don't mean nothing. But for Joe Pentland, he'd be in the pokey. Wanted in three states for poaching, and when it ain't poaching, it's getting so cocky-eyed mean drunk that Jesus couldn't help him!"

Pentland was all red in the face and glaring at me. I didn't say nothing.

"Do *any* damn thing when he's like that! A man like him should stay in the woods with the rest of the animals, that's what I say. Meaner'n a snake."

I was surprised to see him getting so hot about a man, especially before a stranger. "I guess it ain't none of my affair," I said. "I just like the way he takes them dogs."

Floyd was walking slowly down the furrows to the horses, and the niggers let a new pair of dogs out of the rig.

"What in hell you let 'em do *that* for?" yelled Pentland, waving at the fresh dogs. "You know damned well I want

7

to put Buddy and Tex onto the singles so's Mister Webster here can see 'em."

Dewey Floyd looked at Pentland kind of funny. Buster come up behind him. He spoke to Buster, still watching Pentland. "Buster, tell 'em to pull on around and put down Tex and Buddy."

That quiet way of speaking, like there was never anything wrong. He just walked over to his horse and slid the gun into the saddle holster, and Pentland rode out after the dogs. The quail was mostly scattered along a ridge of loblolly pine over at the other side of the cornfield, and I headed after them.

Dewey Floyd rode up alongside. He yanked that stick of his out of the gun holster and took to swatting the dry stalks in half as he rode. His horse was used to that funny sound a stick makes, but mine's ears stuck up sharp, and he was all shivery under the saddle.

"Pentland's all riled about somethin, ain't he?" I said.

"Ain't he." Floyd repeated it softly. He took an extra hard cut at a cornstalk, and my horse jumped sideways. "Take keer on that pony," he said, not looking over. "He don't like no weight back o' the saddle, even yore hand."

"What you keep that stick around for?"

"Don't know for sure. Time I was livin in the woods, I kinda liked the feel of it in my hand."

I know he was looking me over, out from under his hat, and still switching the stick.

"I figger Pentland told you some about me?"

"Yeah. Yeah, he sorta did."

The way he was talking made me feel kind of funny.

"That's okay, Mister Webster, don't trouble yourself none. He allers tells ever'body right off 'bout how he's the las' thing 'tween me and damnation." He laughed quietly, still looking at me the way a coon looks out of a tree. "He ain't told you nothin that ain't so, I guess. A feller'd never catch on that him and me's brother-in-laws. Maybe he ain't told you that part yet."

"Nope. What I mean is, you don't have to tell me nothin."

"I reckon I don't, no. Don't pay me no mind, Mister Webster, I jes feels like talkin. Thing is, my sis has got herself married off to this here Pentland, and that's how come I'm here. They don' want no poacher fer kin to the bes' dog trainer in Georgia, which folks say Pentland is, and so they took me on long as I'd keep my nose clean. He's worryin hisself to death about that."

He laughed again. "Never knew a Yankee yet wasn't worryin on *somethin*," he added.

"It looks like you're doin a good job," I said.

"Eatin's good. Job don't pay nothin to speak of, and it ain't news that me and Pentland got no use fer the other. Hell, I'd go back to the woods but fer the dawgs. I'm gittin mighty attached to them dawgs. How'd that li'l Sadie 'pear to you?"

"She's good. You handled her good."

Floyd nodded his head. "She's a right fine dawg, Sadie is. I done all the work on her and I'd like a lot to have her fer mine. These two ain't bad neither."

We were coming up behind Pentland. The sun was right back of the pines in front of us, so bright I could only just make out the dogs. They were close to twenty yards apart, both on nice points.

"Two sets of birds," said Floyd.

Pentland walked in fast, yelling at the setters to hold. He

9

flushed two birds over the near dog, taking one, and swung over and killed a single that got up wild in front of the other dog after the first shot. He made it look harder than Floyd did, but a nice double all the same. Then he was yelling again, dead, dead, and they found the birds fast, only they brought 'em right over to Dewey Floyd.

"What do you want to go calling 'em in like that for?" Pentland hollered at Floyd. "Dammit, you're going to fix these dogs so's they'll come to nobody else!"

He come stomping over toward us, Buster behind him.

"He didn't call 'em, Mister Pentland," I said, kind of uneasy.

"Seems like them ol' dawgs jes took a min' to come to Mistuh Dewey Floyd," whispered Buster, looking scared, and then Floyd had his horse over between Buster and Pentland.

"You, Buster, get to hell back to them wagons," Floyd said. He cut Buster's horse across the rump with his stick, and the nigger lit out down the ridge and over the cornfield, all arms and legs and flapping leather.

That was it, right there. Talking soft and slow all the time, nice as hell to the dogs and niggers, and then he takes and cuts a horse like that.

Floyd didn't look at Pentland at all. He come back past me, grinning a funny grin, and saying, "Look at that nigger boy ride, Mister Webster, jes you look at that nigger boy ride."

Then he was trotting away, switching his stick in the dew grass, and the dogs right on his heels.

Pentland jammed his gun back in its saddle holster. He wasn't saying a thing. I turned my horse back, and pretty soon he caught up. He was glaring like I was supposed to say something.

10

"I'd like to get a look at some more dogs," I said.

The rest of the day there wasn't much trouble, and I got to see the whole of both rigs. I never seen two men handle dogs like Floyd and Joe Pentland; there wasn't much to be said between them except they run the dogs different ways. Maybe it come from being a poacher, but Floyd knew the country like he was a part of it, and right where the birds was every time. That takes a man that's lived in the woods alone.

I GOT BACK THERE a few weeks later with an order for the three best setters Pentland was selling and the lemon bitch pointer if I could get her.

You could see right away that things was different. Dewey Floyd was leaning against the stable like before, switching dust with the stick, and there was the nigger right beside him. I didn't know it was Buster right off because he didn't have no boots, and niggers generally look pretty much the same. But he said "Mawnin, Mistuh Webstuh," and I knew it was him, only he sure looked different without the boots.

Dewey Floyd peered out from under his hat.

"Mornin," I said. "I come to take that lemon bitch away from you."

"No you ain't." He said it like it didn't need no explanation.

Buster stared at Floyd, kind of fidgety. "Mistuh Webstuh, we-uns ain't wid de dawgs no mo'."

"Buster, you go on up to the house, tell 'em Mister Webster come, you hear me?"

Buster shambled off, looking back over his shoulder. Floyd watched him go.

"Looks kinda sorry without them boots, now don't he?"

11

"What happened?"

"Hell, I don't know. One night las' week I lit into some rotgut, some o' thet sour mash, and come back here and—well, there was a kind of a ruckus, and now me'n Buster is workin here in the stable." Floyd was staring at the ground all the time, kind of tired and tight, watching the end of the stick fooling in the dust.

"I'm sorry to hear it. I sure liked the way you run them dogs."

Joe Pentland was coming down the road to the stable. Floyd was watching him all the time he was talking.

"You see, Mister Webster, a man like me ain't got no place with dawgs. A man what would do what I done, he's a sight better off in the woods. Some of these days I aim to go back, 'cause when I'm here, ain't nothin seems to go right."

Pentland said good morning. "I'm going right down to the pens and get them setters for you, Webster."

He went ahead, then stopped and looked at Floyd. "You ain't paid to lean on that wall, but since you're so busy shooting off your mouth, why not tell Mister Webster why I can't sell him the pointer? Why don't you tell him that?"

Pentland turned to me. "You remember the dog I mean. Sadie. The dog *Mister* Floyd liked so well. Come home here drunk and beat her to death with that damn stick there." He spat on the ground and walked off.

I didn't feel much like looking at Dewey Floyd right then, so I looked at the ground. All I could see was the stick switching back and forth, back and forth, in the dust in front of his shoes. It made me jumpier'n hell, and I glanced up at him. I saw his face. And I'm tellin you right now, it ain't that nigger boy beat Pentland to death, I don't care *what* they say.

12

Floyd was looking after Pentland in that funny way of his, not angry at all, just sort of funny. He went right on talking as if Pentland had never come by, but he didn't take his eyes off him a minute. "You see, I was mighty close to all them dawgs, and that li'l one were my fav'rit. Sadie were a real stylish dawg. I jes don't know rightly what it was, how I could come to doin it. But I did it, sure'n hell."

Dewey Floyd put his stick up under his arm and took out some paper and tobacco. He was talking so quietly I could hear the soft blowing and shifting of the horses through the wall behind him.

"Sober," he said, "I couldn't take this stick to no dawg that way, no more'n I could a pony nor a nigger. But a man . . ."

He paused a minute to fix the tobacco in his cigarette.

"Now you take a man . . . Time comes, I reckon I could do that easier'n nothing." He ran his tongue along the sticking edge of the paper, squinting out at me from under his hat.

1951

THE
FIFTH
DAY

The morning of the fifth day, Dave Winton eased the dragging hook over the side for the last time, wincing at the *thunk* of the twin hook tossed heavily into the water on the other side of the boat and the vicious hum of the outgoing line sawing back and forth over the gunwales. Joe put his hook out that way because it was easy, but to Dave the method made an uneasy difference: Joe's hook, if only because of the haste with which it plunged each morning into the bay, was the one which was certain to seek out the body.

Dave secured his line around the middle seat and turned to the older man for instructions. Joe Robitelli was already settled comfortably in the stern, just as he had been for four days: he hadn't even changed his shirt. The oars lay untouched on the floor of the dinghy.

"Want me to start, Joe?"

"Start what?"

"The oars. We have to keep dragging, don't we?"

"Picket boat's gone, ain't it?" Joe shrugged his shoulders and lay back.

"You said that the drowned man always shows up on the fifth day."

"That's right. Today or tomorrow, or for sure the day after." Joe dragged a small canvas bag from beneath his head. "Look," he said, "Good Old Joe finally got wise to hisself." He hauled two hand lines and a wet bait package out of the bag and spread them triumphantly on the stern seats. "How about that, Dave? And I got six cans of beer to go with it. A regular fishin party."

"You said we were sure to find the guy today."

"Take it easy, kid. Relax. Have a Pabst Blue Ribbon Beer."

"Okay," Dave said, "that was fine the first four days, but sooner or later, we're supposed to find this guy. Maybe we're on top of him right now."

"Look, we ain't supposed to do nothin but sit here, so we might as well have a good time for ourselves. If the guy comes up, the guy comes up, but while we're waitin, I robbed some bacon from the galley for bait and got us six beers from the lighthouse boys."

Dave watched him rig some bacon rind onto the hooks. Joe, glancing at him, winked and sang mournfully, "We three—are all a-lone—" with pointed emphasis on the "three," and winked again. Dave bent over the oars to hide the irritation in his expression; they were pressed against the side of the boat by Joe's ankle. "What's up, Joe?"

15

"What's up, Dave?" Joe studied the baited hooks, his brows wrinkled in concentration.

"Look, I'll do the rowing if you don't want to."

Joe glared back at him. Their faces were uncomfortably close in the drifting boat. "Look, kid, I been tellin you Christ's sake relax for four days now, and here I got you all fixed up with fish lines and beer, and you're still bitchin!"

"What about those people waiting on shore? What do you want to do, keep them waiting all week?"

"It don't *matter* what I want to do, they're gonna wait anyway. So take it easy."

Dave stared at the water eddying silently around the dragging line. He thought about those gloomy people on the pier in their vacation clothes. Right now the hooks were fumbling along the belly of the bay like two clubfeet, scraping and turning and raking the seaweed off the rocks in search of the drowned man. This very moment they could be pulling through the rotten clothes like fingernails through soggy paper.

Joe was leaning back, arms spread and a fish line in each hand, his white cap over his eyes and a cigarette loose in his mouth.

"I guess I'll row awhile, just for the hell of it," Dave said.

Joe shrugged his shoulders and took his foot away from the oars, then hitched one of the fish lines around a cleat and pushed the cap back with the free hand, unveiling a stare of disbelief.

"What in hell are you provin, Davey Boy?"

"Nothing." Dave licked his lips. "I just don't feel right about those people ashore, I guess."

"I don't give a good goddamn *how* you feel about them people ashore. Didn't the Old Man tell em go home and wait, but no, they gotta camp out here and raise a stink till we find him. They'd be yellin at us to get out here if there was a hurricane goin on, especially the ones like you, with a lot of dough and no sense. All we're out here for is to make em happy thinkin we're doing somethin, understand? We ain't even got a outboard motor."

Joe sucked violently on his cigarette.

"The Old Man hisself wouldn't act no different than what I'm doing. I been at this game a long time, and you ain't nothin but a kid, I don't care how much dough you got, just remember that."

There was nothing to offer in defense of a wealthy family. Dave pulled the oars quietly. Joe was still glaring at him as the tension evaporated between their faces.

Then Joe laughed shortly, pulling his cap back over his eyes. "Look, Dave, all I'm sayin is, this bay's six miles across, and all we got is two lousy draggin hooks and a ten-foot dinghy. There ain't a prayer of findin the guy."

"Okay. Maybe I feel like getting a little exercise."

Joe flicked his cigarette over the side. It stuck on the flat bay water like a leaf on the mud. "Yeah," he said. "That's what you wanna do, Davey, get a little exercise."

DAVE CUT VICIOUSLY at the bland-faced water, and the oar, skating over the surface, arched a leaf of spray onto Joe's shirt. A thick brown hand came up slowly, pushed its fingers over the drops, then drifted upwards to the cap, pushing it back over the forehead. Joe's eyes were bright with suspicion, observing Dave's reddening face. One hazel eye winked in a sleepily patronizing manner before the thick hand rose again, methodic as a derrick, adjusted the cap over the eyes, and fell back over the stern.

Any day but today he might have been a stumpy Italian

fisherman sleeping in the sun, his short legs sprawled in the bottom of any small boat in the world, but today he was a tough Brooklyn guinea with his cap over his eyes and a smelly shirt on his back, who didn't give a damn for the water, the sun, the morning, but especially not for the drowned man softening somewhere beneath them, nor the frightened family in their new vacation clothes who waited for the fifth day on the pier.

Dave spat noisily into the water. It was bad enough rowing around in the sun with two hooks dragging without having to watch a guy like this take it easy three feet away. And worst of all, Joe was right. There was no sense in rowing, no sense at all.

Dave rowed furiously, then rested the oars again. He watched the water drops fall from the blades. The body was sure to be off in the other direction.

Amusement deepened on Joe's face. Dave waited for the brown hand to rise to the cap, then dipped the oars again in the teeth of the smile. But the smile judged him with confidence:

"How you doin, Dave?"

"All right. It's getting kind of hot."

"Yeah, it must be. That's okay, though, long as you're getting your exercise, ain't that right, Dave?"

The smile broadened. Joe pulled a pack of cigarettes out of his breast pocket and flicked one up. Dave refused it with a nod.

"The fish ain't bitin so good." Joe pulled the cigarette from the pack with his lips. "I guess there was plenty to eat the last few days here in the bay."

18   Joe secured the fish lines to the stern cleats and brought

his hands up behind his head, chuckling at the subtlety of the implication.

"Why not boat them oars and take it easy, Davey Boy. You ain't provin nothin."

"I'm not trying to."

"Okay." He was watching Dave pull the oars in over his lap, and Dave, uneasy, drew a cigarette from his own pocket and lit it before he remembered. He glanced at Joe's expression:

First of all you didn't like the fish lines and beer, and now my cigarettes ain't good enough for you, it said.

"I didn't feel like one a minute ago," Dave said. Joe didn't answer. They sat still in the hot boat until he spoke.

"I guess you got a lot of dough in your family, huh, Dave?"

"Lay off, Joe. What difference does it make?"

"No difference. I'm just askin. It ain't nothing to be ashamed of." Joe opened a can of beer without looking at it. "Like this guy we're lookin for, he wasn't ashamed of it. He bought hisself a little boat to take the family joy-ridin."

"So what?"

"So he got hisself drowned." Joe laughed.

"And you're not sorry for those people?"

"Sure I'm sorry. Sorry as hell. Still and all, they shoulda gone home like they was told."

"So we're not going to do a thing."

"Sure. We're gonna float around and look at the scenery until the guy pops up and asks for a beer."

Joe was smiling again, but the corners of his smile pointed down instead of up. Dave shifted on the seat. The sun was hot on his back, and his legs were cramped. What in hell was so funny. From where he sat, Joe's grin looked six inches across. And dumbly, he watched Joe lean forward and lift the oars from the oarlocks and lay them along the gunwales on top of the seats. To resist would be to expose himself again.

He eased himself onto the floorboards in the bow of the dinghy, his back to Joe.

"Atta-boy."

Joe's laugh ruffled through his hair, fell back with a triumphant clatter into the stern. Good Old Joe. One more smile and he'd ram an oar down Good Old Joe's throat. Suppose that family was watching them from shore? Even the drowned man must be waiting for them now. He might be two inches under the dinghy, or rubbing softly against the drifting hull. Perhaps even Joe was nervous about him. Joe said he'd pop up like a rubber ball on the fifth day.

DAVE STIRRED UNCOMFORTABLY, peering at the water of the bay. Not a sound, not even a gull, just the heat and the dry paint smell of the dinghy and Good Old Joe in the stern, nursing plans for someone else's wife. Dave laughed at this idea, and the laugh caused a suspicious stir behind him.

Joe's voice was loud in the silence of the bay. "You hear how it happened?" The tone was innocent.

"How what happened?"

"The rich guy." Joe pronounced the words slowly. "The rich guy that got hisself drowned."

"Oh yeah, the rich guy. The rich guy that got himself drowned." Dave paused. "Well, the way I heard it, Joe, this rich guy bought himself a little boat to take his family joyriding and got himself drowned."

20

nder the noon sun, Dave's rage swarmed through him
fruit flies in a heated jar. He crouched in wait for Joe's
action, afraid at the same time to turn and face it. Joe's
tone, however, conveyed no hint of the wound.

"That's right, Dave. How did it happen?"

"I don't know exactly," he parried. "The guys told me
he tried to make it ashore to get help after they capsized."

"He tried to make it ashore okay, so he could save his
own ass. I guess you thought he was a goddam hero or
somethin."

"Yeah, I guess I did. I guess I thought he was a goddam
hero or something."

"Well he ain't. He run out on his wife and kids." Joe's
voice was suddenly angry. "It's bad enough havin these rich
guys get salty on us and gettin hung up on sand bars and
makin us risk our necks to save theirs, but I never thought
they was all yella."

The words hung in the silence overhead as if unwilling
to drift away over the empty bay.

"Oh sure." Dave nodded his head philosophically.
"That's the thing about rich guys, Joe. You wouldn't believe it, Joe, but all rich guys are yellow. The richer the guy,
the wider the yellow streak, every time."

Dave turned to face Joe, excited to see his smile waver,
fall away entirely.

"Don't get smart with me, Davey Boy. I'm wise to you.
Just don't try that sarcastic shit on me, understand?"

"What's the trouble, Joe?"

"Look, Sonny, I'm warnin you, don't get snotty. You're
lookin for a smack in the mouth'll last you a long time,
understand? So watch yourself."

Dave felt his own smile flutter mournfully on his face.

21

It didn't belong there, not because he was afraid but be[...] the game was over, and now he was suddenly so angry [...] he spoke with difficulty, in a gasping, distant voic[...] "C'mon, Joey Boy, relax. Smile. Laugh. You don't care[...] about the rich guy, you're just out here to lay around and scratch your balls."

Joe didn't hit him, only flipped his beer can over the side and hauled in the fish lines. And aware for the first time of the picket boat coming up behind, Dave groped aimlessly for the bow line. Joe grinned as they rigged the lowered pulley to the dinghy. "It's okay to shoot your mouth off with the boat comin, Davey Boy, but I'm gonna take you up behind the boathouse soon as we tie up."

He watched Joe's raucous reception on the boat, his easy way with the other men. On the return, Dave's anger fizzled away in wide, erratic circles over the bay, like a stray wasp, until it disappeared entirely. The boat was early, he'd made a fool of himself, and he was going to have his head knocked off for nothing. They hadn't even found the drowned man. To hell with him.

He stepped onto the pier and turned to wait for Joe, who stood foremost in a grinning knot of men. Dave sensed that he was expected to act, and turned away. He stopped short at the sight of the corpse.

The water was sliding from the drowned man's clothes and escaping through the slats of the pier. Dave listened to its uneven tick on the dead water around the pilings. The terrible apathy of the carcass only made him wonder why they hadn't wrapped it up in canvas and taken it away before the family arrived. Joe was right: those people should have gone. What could this thing mean to them anymore?

Looking away, he saw the Old Man coming down the

road to the pier, attended by two men with a stretcher, but the breeze, tacking momentarily, shocked him back into the dead man's presence. He stepped away, shouldering Joe.

"That's why they come for us early," Joe said. "The fifth day, just like I told you."

Joe glanced at the bulging mask and turned back to Dave.

"Five days in the water don't do much for a guy." He studied Dave's expression.

"He don't look much like a hero, huh, Dave? Imagine a family hangin around five days to have a look at that."

Dave stared at the face again and sat down abruptly on the edge of the pier. "Leave him alone," he muttered, his voice far away.

"I ain't botherin him one little bit."

When Joe laughed, Dave opened his eyes. He saw the proffered cigarette in the dark hand, but he could not move. Joe tapped the cigarette against the back of the hand.

"Here they come," he said.

They watched the drowned man's family approach the foot of the pier, like a knot of sheep unsure of their footing, then glanced at the stretchermen, who were pushing the body onto a rusty square of canvas.

"Snap it up, you guys, give 'em a break." Joe's tone was urgent under his breath. "C'mon, Dave," he said. He headed down the pier with the picket boat crew.

Dave stood up, but his legs moved uncertainly. The sun was very hot. He watched the other men meet and pass the oncoming family, both groups moving shyly, in single file. Following Joe Robitelli's example, most of the men had removed their caps.

THE CENTERPIECE

In 1941 Grandmother Hartlingen, Madrina to the family, was considerably older than anyone I had ever known, "too old for Christmas presents," as she said. She had given way gently to her years, lowering the window upon her past as on a too early snow, yet thoughtfully aware of its delicate weight on the high eaves of her household.

None of her family lived beneath her roof, nor even in the township of Concord, but they were present nevertheless, in neat smiling ranks upon her bedroom tables, ones and twos and threes, and in various postures of memory throughout the rooms. Most of them would gather for her German Christmas, and the rest had preceded her into the ground. These she had long ago forgiven, they lost no favor on the bedroom tables, represented only a certain unsatisfactory transience, like gypsies or violets.

In the dark December of 1941, I alone among Madrina's descendants suffered no misgivings about her festival. To a boy of fourteen, German Christmas meant receiving presents twelve hours in advance and Christmas Day free to enjoy them, and had nothing whatever to do with Germany.

The relation of Christmas to war seemed as tenuous to Madrina as to myself. She had visited Germany but twice in her lifetime and did not intend to visit there again. At the same time, although she was born in New York City, a heritage of Christmas in Bavaria was imprinted in the first pages of her mind, not only of the Hartlingen gathering itself but of the beauty of this tradition to all Germans, at home or abroad. For Madrina, like a fountain sinking back into its well, had returned unconsciously to her source as she grew older, and had long since astounded her countrymen of Concord by referring to herself as High German. No shell threatened the household of habit her universe had become, and although she crocheted for the soldiers, and was offended by the Red Cross refusal of her offer of blood—good German blood, she assured them—she saw no grounds whatsoever for renouncing her German Christmas. It never occurred to her, in fact. Those of the family to whom it did occur awaited in vain the reprieve from Concord, and finally, not daring open rebellion, forgathered uneasily on Christmas Eve. It was the last German Christmas ever celebrated in our family, for Madrina died late in the following year.

Everybody forgathered, that is, except Cousin Millicent, aged fifteen, who refused to leave the car.

My cousin was known in school as Silly Milly, and, as cousins are apt to be, she was ill-favored and even a little distempered. She contributed to family gatherings her own

25

special brand of lackluster silence, as if life in general were a personal affront and no stratagem on the part of others would make her a party to it. Milly was the last descendant Madrina would have suspected as the viper, and Milly's parents, Uncle Charles and Aunt Alice, were as startled as the rest of us. Milly's teacher in school, her one friend in the world, had lost a brother at Pearl Harbor, and Milly's awareness of the forces of good and evil was far keener than my own. After all, I told her, Madrina isn't celebrating a *Japanese* Christmas.

We had gone to sing Christmas carols in the country church. When the tramping of boots had died in the hallway, and the family, the snow still white on their heads, had picked their way into the living room and paid homage to Madrina, there was a moment of silence for the mutineer.

"Good," Madrina said, taking the census through her lorgnette, attached by a wisp of chain to her collar. I can remember how struck I was by this large matriarchal woman with a full-featured serenity of visage entirely absent in the generations grouped before her. "Good," she repeated, "you've come at last. And where is Millicent?"

"Silly Milly," I remarked, from behind the Christmas tree. I had winnowed my presents from a heap which cornucopiaed from the base of the spruce to the shoulder of the hearth, and was engaged in arraying them in good order for opening. The face of the tree was splendid in red candles, with fine antique ornaments, gilt and silver, garnet and emerald, and Bohemian crystal of the sort Madrina said was no longer made. "Silly Milly," I said, "won't come to German Christmas."

Uncle Charles requested my silence, and Aunt Alice stepped forward.

26

"It's nothing, Madrina," she said, and smiled.

"What? What's nothing? Don't smile at me that way, Alice. Are you ill?"

"Milly's taking a stand," Uncle Charles announced, and I saw my father wince. "I'm sure she'll be in in a while, Madrina."

"Taking a stand? What on earth is he saying?" Madrina seized her lorgnette again and peered at her elder son as at an impostor. "The child is far too young to take a stand on *anything*."

She pronounced "take-a-stand" all in a word, as if Milly, in conspiracy with Uncle Charles, were doing something unheard-of, even a trifle indecent.

"What is it, Charles? Have her come in this instant."

"In a few minutes, Madrina," my father said. "She's being very silly about it."

"Silly Milly," I repeated, vindicated, and was promptly admonished by my sister Polly, the eldest of the younger generation and its unofficial keeper. Madrina's attention was thereby drawn to me.

"Wolfgang," she said, "come out from behind that tree and fetch a candy to your cousin."

"My name's not Wolfgang," I objected, but out I came. Madrina had taken to calling me Wolfgang quite arbitrarily, since my given name is Wendell and my popular title is Sandy. I think Wolfgang satisfied a curious humor of Madrina's devoted to the nettling of my parents. "What candy?" I said.

"What candy, *Madrina*," Polly said. Polly was very tiresome as a child.

"It doesn't matter what candy," my mother said. "Do as you're told, Wendell."

27

"Sandy," I said. I ran into the dining room to look for candy and greet the servants, but was arrested, as I had been every year, by the wondrous centerpiece on the table. It was five feet long, Saint Nicholas and the reindeer before a hostelry, hand-wrought of mahogany and bone, and re-staged each year with cotton-and-mica snow. After a long service in Germany, a century of Hartlingen Christmases, it had been delivered into Madrina's hands, and now symbolized to all of us not only Christmas but the past. It was girded round with pine fronds and holly, the orbit of a vast oval of silverware and banquet oddments, muscat raisins, mints, almonds, wine, cranberry jelly, and butterballs. Madrina had beautiful silver, ancient and heavy with Hartlingen history, the epochs of pigs with apples in their mouths and wine from golden goblets.

I secured a thin mint for Milly, but it deteriorated in transit, and Madrina instructed me to throw it into the fire. "Take one of those," she said, and pointed out a gleaming coffer on a side table, guarded by dancing Dresden figurines, ivory burgomeisters, and a peevish dachshund named Bismark V, decaying on a period chair.

"I hope they're not *German* candies," I said.

"You'd be in luck if they were," Madrina told me, and laughed so oddly that I turned to stare at her. The reason for Milly's stand had obviously been explained, and now my grandmother regarded the family, fourteen strong about the room, with an abstracted gaze, as if they could not be her family after all.

Uncomfortable, I selected the biggest item from the box and hastened through the snow to Milly. Milly had her nose pressed to the rear window of the car, and although she ducked back at my appearance, I knew she was happy someone had come.

"Here, silly," I said.

She struck the candy from my hand.

"Oh-h!" Milly gasped. "That old German thing! I don't love *her* anymore."

"Can I have your candy, then?" I said, picking it up.

"No!" Milly said and, snatching it from me, burst into tears. Now she was uglier than ever, and I had neither the age nor wisdom to be sorry for her. "And I won't come in. I won't!" Her knee, in stamping, knocked the candy into the snow.

"All right," I said, seizing it, "but you're spoiling everything." I ran back up the path, my mission a delightful failure.

The wreathed light from the windows gave body to the darkness, breathing tracery into the slow arras of snow. It gave the house a snug, enchanted air, like some magic sanctuary of childhood deep in a wood. The holly berries on the door wreath, round red as picture peasants' cheeks, and the deep green halo of ground pine itself were as fresh as our New World winter. Inside, the voices traveled on pine-scented air, safe from the future and from Millicent's war.

"Silly Milly lost the candy in the snow and won't come in," I reported, swallowing the last of it.

There was a pause, and eyes turned to Madrina for her dictum.

Madrina said, "How very foolish."

She rang for Clara, who presently appeared with a copper caldron of brandy and milk and nutmeg, and a set of silver mugs. There was a fine bowl of nuts by the fire, black walnuts, butternuts, and hazel nuts, and seated in warmth, one eye cast luxuriously on my presents, I indulged myself in contempt for Milly and pity for Madrina, undone by the rude granddaughter outside.

Seated in her flowered chair as still and enduring as the dry cattails and bittersweet in the vase behind her, her face alive with soft expressive rhythms, like a moment of birds in a winter tree, Madrina told us a tale of another Christmas, another century.

Her German cousin Ernst was traveling with his mother to a Hartlingen Christmas of long ago, and as the carriage was to pass the region of the Black Forest, the coachman advised his passengers of the danger of brigands, then very numerous in the byways. The brigands were captained by a well-mannered man of noble extraction, so it was said, who treated his victims with great courtesy so long as they offered no resistance, but dealt very harshly with objectors. Madrina's cousin Ernst was just the sort to object, he had no sense of humor in such matters, and his mother cautioned him strongly against rash actions in the event of trouble. No sooner had she spoken than the carriage halted, and she was handed down by an enormous bearded gentleman, who relieved her discreetly of all jewelery but a family brooch, of the sentimental value of which she had managed to persuade him. At this moment Ernst sprang from the carriage, brandishing a pistol, and was on the point of *taking a stand* on the matter, Madrina said tartly, when his head, parted from his shoulders by the sword of a mounted henchman, rolled ignominiously under the carriage. Very regrettable, the chieftain remarked, and seized the brooch.

Madrina's aunt was inconsolable. She bent and peered under the carriage, where, catching the eye of her son, she shouted at him: "I told you, Ernst! I told you, you block-head!"

Madrina peered from one descendant to the next, as if seeking a successor by the gauge of laughter. But her own smile faltered, then disappeared entirely. "We shall go to dinner," she whispered. The family stared toward the hall-way, where not Milly but Clara, her hands prim on her apron, leaned sepulchrally into the room. "We will start without Miss Millicent, Clara," Madrina said, less to Clara than to Milly herself, as if she had said, I told you, Ernst, I told you!

Marching past the faded tapestries and bronze-green urns from the halls of her forebears, artifacts far too ponderous for the houses of her children, Madrina entered the dining room, touching the oaken chairs fondly as she journeyed to her place.

"She will come in a minute, Madrina," Aunt Alice said.

"She will do as she pleases," said Madrina.

From my position, far away below the salt, the center-piece stretched eternally between the two lines of heads which converged on the white face of Madrina. She gave a whispered benediction, and afterward the family toasted her, holding high the glasses of Rhenish wine. Against the candlelight and the chandelier, the red wine glowed like liquid rubies, and I was a baron at a medieval board, drunk on the wine of my betters.

When, late in the second course, the centerpiece ignited from a fallen candle, the flame ran a furious circle in the snow before an uncle had the wit to dash his wine at it. The inn was tinder in the molten cotton, and the whalebone reindeer pranced proudly on the table, freed forever of Saint Nicholas, who perished in his sleigh.

In the chaos of motion and voices I saw Madrina, the only person still seated, observing the destruction as if the ruin of this antiquated treasure was somehow fitting, as if she sensed that, like the tapestries and urns, it was far too venerable and vast to serve the New World Hartlingens again.

She did not respond to the condolences addressed to her, but sat in silence, her hands folded on her lap. When at last she could be heard, she said: "Milly . . . I would like to see Milly."

And as if the girl had been poised on the threshold, the door flew open and Milly appeared, in a flurry of snow and tears, stumbling forward to Madrina. Milly cried very loudly in Madrina's embrace, and Madrina was crying, too, a harsh unwilling sputter which her glaring eyes denied.

"It's all my fault," Milly was saying, "it's all my fault."

And Madrina, looking over Milly's shoulder at the black Saint Nicholas, said: "How foolish, my dear. I am as American as you are. We are simply celebrating Christmas Eve."

1951

LATE
IN THE
SEASON

It was just at the edge of the late November road, a halted thing too large for the New England countryside, neither retreating nor pulling in its head, but waiting for the station wagon. Cici Avery saw it first, a dark giant turtle, as solitary as a misplaced object, as something left behind after its season. She nudged her husband and pointed, unwilling to break the silence in the car.

Frank Avery saw the turtle and slowed. If he had been alone, he would have swerved to hit it, Cici decided, selecting the untruth which suited her mood.

The small eyes fastened on the man. The tail, ridged with reptilian fins, lay still in the dust like a thick dead snake, pointing to the yellowed weeds which, leading back over a slight crest and descending thickly to the ditch, were flattened and coated by a wake of mud.

Cici, hands in her trousers, moved in unlaced boots past her husband. The tips of the laces flicked in the dust like broken whip ends.

"Poor monster," she whispered to the turtle. "It's late in the year for you, you're past your season."

"Monster isn't the word," Frank Avery said. "I've never seen such a brute." He ventured a thrust at it with his riding boot. "It's not *really* a turtle?" he said.

"A snapping turtle," Cici said. She was a big untidy girl whose straw-colored hair blurred the lines of her face.

"A man-eater," he said. "It must be two feet across."

"It's a very big old monster," she said, sinking down on the crest behind it and stroking the triangular snout with her stick. The mouth reared back over the shell, its jaws slicing the stick with a leathery thump.

"Dear God!" Frank said.

Cici eased to her elbow in the grass, stretching the long legs in faded hunting pants out to one side of the turtle. She studied her husband. Frank Avery, precise in his new riding habit, stood uncertain beside the bull-like turtle, afraid of it and fascinated at once.

The very way he behaves with me, the thought recurred to her, as if I were some slightly disgusting animal, and yet he prides himself on his technique, which doesn't include having children. Romance is the watchword, but no children, not for a while. And then he is hurt because I don't love him. As if we were haggling over love as the stud fee, as if I had bargained with him for his manhood, she thought, and didn't realize until I took it home what a rotten bargain I had made.

Frank Avery stretched out his toe and sent the turtle sprawling on its back.

"Come on, you coward," he said. "Fight."

The turtle reached back into the dust with its snout and pivoted itself upright with its neck muscles, then heaved around to face the enemy.

"Leave it alone," Cici said. "It can't help being a turtle."

"We should kill it," Frank told her. "It's disgusting."

We should kill it, she thought, because it's harmful on a farm, not for *your* reason. Lying there watching him badger the turtle, she felt a slow hurt anger crawling through her lungs, as if he had injured her over a period of time and only now she understood. She was sorry for the turtle, for its mute acceptance of the riding boots which barred its way.

"You don't have to look at it," she said. "Besides, it's mine. I saw it first."

He turned to her, hands on hips, smiling his party smile.

"A fine thing," he said, and waited for her question.

"What is?" she obliged him, after a moment.

"Here we've been married a year and now it's turtles. First it was kittens and puppies, and then horses, and now turtles. I appreciate your instincts, Cici, but you *can't* get weepy over turtles!"

He laughed sharply.

"Can't I?" she said. Unsmiling, she watched the laugh wither in his mouth.

Frank kicked suddenly at the turtle's head, but his toe shrank from the contact and only arched a wave of dust into the hard stretched mouth and the little eyes. When the turtle blinked, the dust particles fell from above its eyelids.

"Did I ever tell you about Toby Snead, Frank? When the other kids would torture a rat or a frog, Toby Snead would jump around, squealing and giggling. He loved it.

35

He was skinny and weak, and he loved to see them pick on something besides himself."

"Was I giggling?" Frank said. His face was white.

I've gone too far, Cici thought, and I'm going to go farther. She felt exhausted, lying back in the natural grass, easing herself of a year of disappointment as calmly as a baby spitting up cereal, a little startled by the produce of its mouth, yet more curious than concerned.

"And you'll get your manly new boots dirty, Frank," she murmured.

"I haven't been here every year to get them faded," he said. When she didn't answer, he added, "And pick up a local accent, and ogle the hired hand."

"The caretaker, you mean," Cici said, her eyes on the turtle. He's jealous, she thought, actually jealous; he can't admit that *he* made a rotten bargain, too.

"Oh Cici, let's skip it," Frank said. "I don't know what's the matter with you these days."

"I hope you find out," Cici said, turning her eyes on him, "before my change of life."

"Let's not start *that* all over again," Frank Avery said. His voice was tight, a little desperate. "I'm sick of it. And you'll catch cold, sitting on the ground."

"There's plenty between me and the ground," Cici said, grinning. She rose and, turning her buttocks to him, brushed the grass off with both hands.

"See?" she said, over her shoulder. "Besides, I've got *you* to keep me warm."

She stepped around the turtle and, taking Frank's face between her hands, kissed him with exaggerated sensuality on the mouth. When he tried to embrace her, however, she slipped from him.

"Cici, listen to me," he said, but she refused, stooping to the turtle.

"C'mon, monster," she said. "I'll take you home and mother you."

"Permit me," Frank said, and clowned a bow, but his heart was not in it. Circling behind the turtle, he seized it convulsively by the rear edges of its carapace and bore it like a hot unbalanced platter to the car.

"What do you want him for?" he said. Then, "Open the door, will you?"

"Monster's peeing on you," Cici told him, laughing in a way which suggested an alliance with the turtle against him. Watching his face, she was sorry she had laughed, but not for Frank's sake. Frank was an artist at revenge, he much preferred it to the messy temper which came to Cici so naturally. She knew him now, and would expect reprisal.

The turtle blundered to the rear of the station wagon and pressed its snout against the backboard. Alarmed by this detour in its life, it scraped its claws like harsh fingernails over the metal floor.

"Let's let it go, Frank," Cici said, afraid.

"No, no," Frank insisted. "I'm sure Cyrus would like to see it."

Indoors, the turtle looked double its size. Cyrus Jone's boy Jackie had never seen anything like it. He trapped the turtle in the kitchen corner and dropped marbles on its head until Cici asked him to stop. Mrs. Jone, thin-armed in a cotton print, rushed over and slapped him in deference to Mrs. Avery.

Cyrus nodded shortly at Cici as if to excuse his remark, and said to his wife, "Not much sense in slappin the boy if you ain't spoken to him first. He ain't a dog."

37

"I can't have him pesterin folks," she whined, retreating to the stove.

Cyrus Jones did not answer her. He said to Cici, "Your father telephoned, Miss Cici, he's comin down tomorrow."

"Oh, that'll be nice," squeaked Mrs. Jone.

"Yes," Cici said. She was holding a baby Jone on her lap while its mother, one eye on the turtle, rummaged nervously with the supper.

Jackie, a large-headed child with prominent ears, goaded the turtle furtively. It renewed its effort to penetrate the corner.

"That's enough, Jackie," his father told him.

"I ain't doin nothin! I just wanted to see if he was all right!"

"He's all right," Cyrus said. He was a big man of strong middle age, whose hands rested tranquilly on his knees. His eyes were restless, however, and Cici knew he was watching her from the shadow of his corner. She glanced at his wife, already pressing a new round belly to the stove.

Frank Avery came into the kitchen. In his left hand he carried a .22 pistol, which he placed in the corner of the sideboard, in his right the whisky bottle from their suitcase. It was not quite full, Cici noticed.

"I'll have your dinner in a minute, Mr. Avery," Mrs. Jone said. Her eyes switched rapidly from the bottle to the turtle to the pistol, coming to rest at last on Frank's forehead.

"Why don't we all eat together?" Cici said.

"And Cici can hold the baby," Frank said to her.

Cici did not return his smile, and only Jackie said, "Sure, we kin all eat together and watch the turtle."

"That's right," Frank said. "We might have a cocktail beforehand."

"I'm sure you folks'd rather . . ." Mrs. Jone began, terrified.

"What are you gonna do with the pistol?" Jackie demanded, touching it.

He's been drinking upstairs, Cici thought. I'll never placate him now, and I've missed my chance to let the turtle go. She had forgotten the turtle, she knew it did not matter to her, but suddenly its survival seemed urgent.

"Whatever you folks want'll do fine for us," Cyrus said. He rapped his fingers on his knees.

"Hey, what are you gonna do with the pistol?" Jackie repeated.

"Mr. Avery," Mrs. Jone corrected him.

"Mr. Avery," Jackie said.

But Frank had gone to the pantry for ice. He returned in a moment with four glasses of it.

"Great," he said, pouring out the whisky.

In the moment of silence, the turtle pushed upward against the wall, then fell back heavily to the floor.

"Jackie wants to know what you're going to do with the pistol," Cici said.

"I was just about to ask Cyrus," Frank said. He passed the glasses and sat down.

"What's that, Mr. Avery?" Cyrus said.

"That turtle, Cyrus. I understand that kind of turtle is harmful, eats fish and young ducks and things."

"Frogs, mostly. That's right, though."

"Dangerous to swimmers, I imagine."

"I don't guess so. They're pretty leery, them hogbacks."

"Frank wants to kill the turtle, Cy," Cici said.

39

"Sure, let's kill'm!" Jackie said. "We kin shoot him with the pistol."

"Shush, Jackie," hissed Mrs. Jone. When Cici glanced at her, she hid her whiskey glass among the pots on the back of the stove.

"I don't *want* to kill it, darling," Frank said. "I just don't think we should let it go."

"That's too bad, *dar*ling," Cici told him. "Because it's my turtle. I found it, and I'm going to let it go."

Her anger was sudden and quiet. The little boy watched her, open-mouthed, and Cyrus said, "I guess I'd ha' killed it, had I found it, Miss Cici."

"You didn't find it, though," Cici snapped.

"You're being childish about it, Cici," Frank said.

"No, I didn't, that's true." Cyrus laughed, as if Frank's interruption were of no more consequence than the turtle's bumping in the corner. "But there's not much good in a critter like that."

"That's right," Frank Avery said. Prematurely, he refilled all the glasses but Cici's, which was untouched, and now sat down again. "We all agree it should be killed, Cici."

"I ain't sayin *that*," Cyrus said. "I don't guess one turtle could do much harm on a place this size, although I'd just as soon be rid of it."

The baby was stirring now in Cici's arms.

"I'll take it upstairs," Cici said, over the protests of Mrs. Jone. Her face, pressed to the baby's head, softened again to its usual fullness, but her mouth was set, and she did not look at her husband as she rose.

"Cici loves babies," Frank's voice said, pursuing her to the back stairway; it was followed by a laugh. "Babies and turtles."

Mrs. Jone's giggle tinkled like the cheap alarm clock over the pots on the stove.

She was still giggling when Cici returned and sat down to dinner.

"I *do* love babies, yes," Cici said to Frank.

"Well, I must say they're a terrible trouble," Mrs. Jone told her. "You don't know your own luck, Mrs. Avery."

"We have a baby every year," Jackie announced, but his mouth was already so occupied that nobody understood him except his mother.

She said, "Jackie!" and blushed.

Cyrus watched his wife, chewing his dinner without expression.

The turtle had found its way out of the corner and was dragging itself along the wall in the direction of the kitchen door. Cici listened. The belly plate touched the floor on alternate steps, a dull pendulum rhythm of tap and suspense which went unnoticed at the table.

"Yes, they'd certainly be trouble in *my* work, with all the traveling I do," Frank was saying.

"Oh, you'll have them, though, Mr. Avery," said Mrs. Jone. "Never you fear. Why, it's only nature."

"It's only nature, Frank." Cici grinned.

"Of course we will." Frank Avery frowned. Unlike Mrs. Jone, he had brought his whisky to the table. "Right now, of course, it's inconvenient, but there's plenty of time. We're only thirty."

Cici did not comment, she had heard it all before, and to her it rang false and unnatural. As her time diminished, she had settled for Frank Avery and children. She had wanted to love him so badly, and now, in secret ways, he punished her because she could not. Having settled for less,

41

she was to be cheated of that, too. It was all Cici could do to swallow, and sorry for herself, she permitted her eyes to cloud with tears.

She wondered if Catholic Mrs. Jone had been offended by his tactlessness. But Mrs. Jone was obviously too stimulated to be offended by anything, and Cici looked at Cyrus, who was now intent on the turtle's progress along the wall.

Very quietly, without turning toward her, Cyrus said, "His pond must have dried out on him, he's after a new mud to winter in, this late in the year."

Cici nodded. The turtle had exposed itself to trouble.

She watched her husband, who had heard Cyrus's voice but lost the words in the clatter of Jackie's fork, and was now glancing from one to the other with a half-smile, as if he wished to be included.

The turtle was directly behind him.

Cici did not enlighten her husband, offering instead a wink of innocence and duplicity which brought new color to his face. He glared expectantly at Cyrus, but Cyrus was absorbed with his mashed potatoes and did not notice.

Frank rose abruptly and went into the pantry for more ice.

Moving quickly, Cici horsed the turtle over the floor and out the kitchen door into the darkness, straining the precious seconds in her effort to be quiet.

"Oh boy," Jackie said, rising. "Let's go!"

"Be quiet," his father told him, his eyes on Frank Avery, who returned as Cici sat down. Frank's face was red with irritation, and he only glanced at her questioningly.

Cici smiled at him and said nothing. Her heart pounding, she cheered the turtle toward the bushes. The success of her coup was overpowering: like a schoolgirl, she was forced to bite on the insides of her cheeks to keep from laughing, trembling joyfully in the escape as in a childhood game of hide-and-seek.

"But it'll get away," Jackie whispered to his father, turning away sharply as if he hadn't meant to whisper it, it had just popped out, and therefore he was not to be blamed.

"My mashed potatoes are quite nice and fluffy tonight, if I *do* say so," preened Mrs. Jone, and dropped her fork.

"But listen . . ." Jackie started.

Frank shifted his gaze to Cyrus, who, chewing placidly, returned it.

"When we're finished dinner," Frank said to Jackie, "we'll have to kill the turtle."

"I'm finished now," Jackie blurted. "It's goin to get away."

And then there was silence. Finally, Frank Avery said, "Where in hell did it get to, Cici?"

"I let it go." The laughter jerked from her mouth.

"The turtle?" Mrs. Jone said. She stared at the empty corner.

"That was silly of you, Cici," Frank said. He was trying to control his voice. "You knew it should have been killed."

"Oh, relax, Frank," she said. "It doesn't matter."

"It *does* matter, damn it."

They watched him rise and take the pistol and, followed by Jackie, step out into the darkness.

"Jackie," his mother said.

Cici rose and went to the door. "Frank," she called.

He came back into the light. "I need a flashlight," he

43

muttered. Behind him, Jackie's voice rang through the darkness.

"Frank, don't. Please," she whispered. "It was mine. You're just killing it to spite me."

"You shouldn't have let it go," he said, pushing past her. "You've tried to make a fool of me all day."

When he came back through the kitchen, Cyrus watched him without speaking, but Mrs. Jone whispered, "It's only just a turtle, everybody. Your dinner'll get cold."

Frank grinned tightly, saying to Cyrus, "We shouldn't let it go."

In the door, Cici blocked his way.

"You're being ridiculous, Frank. You're drunk. And who found the turtle? It's mine."

"Goddamnit," he said. "You knew I wanted that turtle killed."

"Why?" she demanded. "Why? Since when are you so interested in ducks and fish and things? They've kept going pretty well so far without any help from you, or the little boy you drag in to keep your courage up."

"You know . . ." he started, but did not bother to go on, because Jackie had found the turtle.

Defeating its own escape, it was pushing against the center of the nearest bush, its legs braced in the dirt. From the doorway, Cici saw Frank's dark hand reach across the flashlight beam and grasp the spiny tail.

Sick, she turned back into the kitchen. When Cyrus rose and went out, she snapped at Mrs. Jone, "How can you sit there and let that little boy watch him?"

Mrs. Jone ran outside.

The shots came slow and uneven—one, twothree, four. The fourth shot drove Cici to the door.

The turtle was moving slowly in the dim light from the kitchen. Frank's back was to her, and through the excited shouts of the little boy and the shrilling of his mother, she heard a quieter sound.

"What are you laughing at?" she said, her voice hushed, but he was pointing the pistol again, leaning back, stiff-armed.

The turtle jerked a little, kept on moving away. One of its hind legs was paralyzed, and there were three black holes in the ancient shell.

"What are you laughing at?" Cici screamed, and the boy Jackie ran into the house after his mother.

"I'm sorry, darling," Frank's voice came. "I know it's not funny, but my shooting's terrible. I can't seem to hit its head. I must be drunk."

"It's still moving," Cici whispered, as he turned to her. "You bastard. You perfect bastard."

Cyrus came around the corner from the garage. He had a hatchet in his hand and stopped the turtle with his boot. It opened its mouth but could not close it again.

"Hell, mister, that's no way to kill a hogback," Cyrus said.

He bent and guillotined the turtle as Cici cried out.

The blood was black on the ground beneath the door light. Cyrus lobbed the head with its still-open mouth out of the light, then hoisted the carcass by the tail and, holding it away from him, moved toward the bushes. Its hind feet were still walking away.

Crying now, Cici slumped in the doorway. Frank Avery tried to approach her.

"It's still moving," she whispered. "You coward. You couldn't even kill it."

45

"Cici, listen," he started.

"I hate you," Cici told him. "You're disgusting."

The turtle fell in the invisible underbrush, a heavy breaking crash which jarred the nighttime into silence.

The returning steps of Cyrus Jone came from the darkness. Behind, the bright-lit kitchen waited, the empty chairs at angles to the cooling dinner. From an upper room, the little boy was crying.

1953

TRAVELIN MAN

Nowember on the Carolina coast is
cold at night, a dark clear cold that kills the late mosquitoes.
Toward dusk, a black man slithered from a drainage
ditch. He moved swiftly on his belly, writhing out across
a greasy bog and vanishing into the sawgrass by the river.
The grass stirred a moment and was still. A rail bird rattled
nervously, and a hunting gull, drawn inland, cocked a
bright, hard, yellow eye. Startled, it dropped a white spot
on the brown waste of the bog and banked downwind.
Deep River is dark with piedmont silt and without depth
or bottom. It bends its way to its wide delta like a great
dead snake slung out across the tidewater, and in the sum-
mertime it smells. Alluvial ooze packed tight and rotting
on its banks sucks into itself the river debris. Through the
grasses near the rim, Traver could see the stranded tree limbs

and the prow of the derelict skiff glimpsed earlier in the day.

It was near dark. Raising his eyes to the level of the grass, he listened a last time. Then he slid forward and, on his knees in the shallows, wrenched the buried skiff from its sheath of mud. It came with a thick sucking sound and the rank breath of its grave.

Traver knew without experiment that, upright, the skiff would fill immediately. He turned it turtle and waited one moment more, gaining his wind. It was high water, the first of the ebb. The tide and river would be with him. He shivered, moaning softly, though not yet afraid.

In the water, he kicked away from shore. An eddy curled him back upon the bank. He kicked away a second time, and caught the current. But the slimy hulk would not support his weight, and he coasted along beside it, one hand spread-fingered on the keel.

He moved downstream. Across the marsh, the lights switched back and forth like nighttime eyes, dancing in the blackness of the pines. The voices came vaguely on the shifting river air, and a new sound stirred him. He sank lower in the water, so that only his hand and half his face broke the low outline of the skiff.

Dey gone and put de hounds on dat man Traver.

He giggled, teeth chattering, and cursed.

The river dragged the capsized skiff across the coastal waterway, which parted the mainland from the inner marshes of the barrier islands. Though wisps of cloud at times obscured the moon, the night was clear. No longer able to see the lights, he was alone in the cold river, which widened now as it neared its mouth. He thrashed his legs for warmth, and cursed to restore his courage. Southeast, an arm of woods from Ocean Island reached across the outer marshes toward the bank. He wanted to go aground there and, fearful of drifting past it to the open sea, began to swim the skiff inshore. To keep himself company, he swore foully at the balky hulk, the cold, the river, the night world.

His voice wandered in the thin mist over the river, and startled by it, he had a cold premonition of his death. But an inshore current seized the skiff and swept it in beneath the bank. Nearing the piles of the abandoned landing, he forsook the skiff and struggled through the shallow water. He had to drag himself ashore. Crouched beneath the wharf, too weak to beat his arms, he listened to hoarse, painful breaths he could not stop. The skiff disappeared around the final bend, toward the booming where the seas broke on the bar.

Traver scraped coon oysters from the pilings and opened them with his knife. Since the clothes he wore were the property of the state, this knife was his sole possession. He had had it fifteen hours. The knife was long, with a spring blade, and when he had eaten, he cleaned it before replacing it in his pocket.

Then he rose, peering over the bank at the trees a hundred yards away. Though sure he was alone on Ocean Island, he disliked outlining himself against the river. He went forward in a low crouch, covert, quiet. He liked to think he was quiet as an animal.

In the shelter of the live oaks, for the first time since early morning, he stood straight. Stretching, he threw his shoulders back, legs spread in unconscious arrogance. Traver was a tall man and very strong, with the big hands and haunches of his race. His skin was the mud black of the coastal Gullah, and his left eye was obscured by scars which extended in cordy ridges toward the neat, tight ear. The scars seemed to have stretched the skin, which was taut and smooth, like a rubber mask. The expression of the mask was open, almost smiling, the boyish smile of a man enjoying himself without quite knowing why.

Most of the time, this smile was genuine. Traver liked to laugh and, though good-natured, he also liked to fight. He had been fighting since the day when, brought home to Raccoon Creek by a wayward mother, he was nicknamed Traveler.

> His Daddy was a Travelin Man
> Traveled away and left his Mam.

The name became Traver, and stayed with him. And he had traveled north, south, east, and west, in and out of work and jail. He could stay no longer in a job than out of trouble. He had worked on the railroad and the road gang and the big menhaden boats out of Hampton Roads, and everywhere he laughed like hell and finally fought. Every once in a while, half-drunk, he would come home. And his mother would tell him, You born with too much life in you, dass all, you like you daddy. And you headin straight fo' trouble, big mule as you is.

The last time home he had fought the man who happened to marry his girl. The man had knifed him near the eye. Unable to catch him, Traver, still bleeding, had burned their cabin down and taken the willing girl away. The sheriff followed in his own good time. I got your old place on the road gang saved for you, the sheriff said. We ain't had a good laugh since you left.

But now, a month later, he had escaped. He appeared with the knife in Raccoon Creek, but the man had moved away. The girl's mother reported him, and he took to the woods, and kept on going out across Deep River Marsh. The tide was flooding when he saw the skiff, and he'd had to wait. He had scurried, crouched, scurried again, and once submerged, sliding beneath the surface like an alligator. The rasping voices had not picked up his trail in the green, broken scum, and they had passed.

I a big bull gator, he sang now, a tough-hide long-tail mean ol' gator. Opening his open mouth a little more, he chortled soundlessly, still shivering. It growin cold, and dis gator ain't no place to warm hisself. Well, I mean. Cold.

He moved inland through the trees, away from the dark river.

Ocean Island is long and large, spreading down some four miles from the delta, southwest toward Cape Romaine. The true land is a narrow spine supporting red cedar, cypress, yaupon, live oak, and the old-field pine, and here and there a scattering of small palmettos. There are low ridges and open groves and clearings, and a core of semi-tropic woods. Its south flank is salt marsh and ocean beach, and to the north, diked years ago above the tide, lies a vast brackish swamp. The swamp is grassy, like a green-and-golden flooded plain, its distances broken by lone, bony trees and hurricane dikes and sluice gates. Here, in a network of overgrown canals, the nut and widgeon grass grows in abandoned rice fields. Wildfowl winter in a diadem of reedy ponds, and coot and rail and gallinule, and predators.

In the swamp, the predators move ceaselessly.

He went to Snake-house. This was a sagging toolshed near the landing, so-called because in other times a worker had been bitten there, and died. In the dark, a sign, NO

51

TRESPASSING, loomed white and new. The door was gone, but the dank interior gave shelter from the breeze. Traver stripped and wrung his clothes, then rubbed his body fiercely with his hands. He found an oily piece of old tarpaulin and, wrapping himself in it, dozed a little, fitful.

He had come to Ocean Island because here he could survive. As a boy he had labored on the rice fields and the dikes, and he knew the name and character of every pond and ditch and slough. He knew where to snare rabbits, stalk birds, ambush deer, and where the wild swine and cattle were which he might outwit and kill. On the salt shores there were razor clams and oysters, and mullet in the canals, if a fish trap could be rigged. He would not starve. He could eat raccoon and otter and, if necessary, he could eat them raw.

He could survive here, too, because he would not be caught. The island had been unused for years, even for gunning. If he was tracked to this forsaken place, he could always find shelter in the swamp. Hounds could not help them here, and the whites did not know the swamp as he did, how to move quickly in it without risking the deep potholes and soft muck. He could elude a wider search than the state would send into the swamp after a black man. For this was black man's country, slow and silent, absorbing the white man's inroads like a sponge. A white man loomed large on Ocean Island, but a black man was swallowed up in it, and disappeared.

IN THE NIGHT, he was awakened by the grunting of a hog. The grunt was nervous, and there was a skittish stamping of small cloven hooves. He smell me, Traver thought. Taking his knife, he glided to the doorway. Upwind, the hog came toward him on the island path. He crouched, prepared to ambush it, then stiffened.

Ol' Hawg scairt. And he ain't scairt of Traver.

Traver stooped for his shirt and pants and slipped outside. The hog snorted and wheeled, crashing off into the brush. Traver slid down a sandbank behind Snake-house and lay watching. He heard a rush of bait fish by the landing, the choked cry of a night heron behind him. A barred owl hooted and was answered. This was the hunting time.

The man had not seen Traver. He had stopped short at the crashing of the hog. Now he came on, down the soft sand path toward Snake-house. He was a tall, lean man with a rifle slung over one arm and a flashlight, unlit, in the other hand. His face was shadowed in the moonlight by his hat brim, turned down all the way around.

Traver opened the knife blade and lay still. He could not retreat now without being seen, and if he was seen, he was lost. He had no doubt that this man was his enemy, an enemy as natural as a raccoon to a frog, nor did it occur to him to curse his luck that an enemy was here at all. He was only relieved that he had heard in time. The rest no longer mattered. Traver was hardened to hunting and being hunted, and the endless adaptation to emergencies. He was intelligent and resourceful, and he was confident. Through the grasses, he gauged the stranger as he passed.

From the man's belt, behind, hung a hatchet and a piece of rope. The rifle, carried loosely, was ready to be raised, and the unlit light was also ready. He was hunting. He crossed a patch of dry grass without a sound, and Traver nodded ruefully in respect.

Dat a poacher. Might be he jackin deer.

The man went on, down toward the landing. Stooping

on the wharf, he peered beneath it. Traver, who had moved, could see him do this, and felt a tightening in his chest.

He see dem feetprints. He see white places where dem orster was. You a plain fool nigger, man.

The hunter returned, moving more quickly. Raising his rifle, he flicked his light into the Snake-house. Traver could see its gleam through the rotting tongue-and-groove.

Ain't no deer in dar, Boss, ain't no deer in dar.

He repressed a nervous giggle, sweating naked in the cold, and clutched his knife. Upwind, he could hear the hog again, rooting stupidly near the path. The white man turned, bent to one knee, and fired. Traver jumped. The report ricocheted across the grove as the hog kicked, squealing, and lay still.

Ol' white folks, he kin shoot. Only why he shootin now and not before? He lookin to fool somebody, he makin pretend he doan know somebody here.

He know, all right. Ol' white folks know.

The man dragged the hog into the trees and dressed it quickly, viciously, with the hatchet and a knife. Then he piled brush on the head and hooves and entrails and, rigging a sling with a length of rope, hoisted the carcass to his shoulder. He went away as silently as he had come, and Traver followed.

We stickin close as two peas, man. I got to know what you up to every minute, lest you come sneakin up behind me.

Traver, though uneasy, was excited, jubilant. It seemed to him that he had won some sort of skirmish, and he could scarcely wait to see what would happen next. But because he guessed where the man was going, he kept a safe distance behind. There was a clearing at Back-of-Ocean, and the old cabin of an abandoned shooting camp, and the only beach on the south side steep enough to bring a boat ashore. The poacher would have to have a boat, and he probably had a helper. Realizing this, Traver slowed, and put on his wet clothes.

He circled the clearing and came in from the far side, on his belly. There was kerosene light in the cabin window, and hanging from its eaves on the outside logs were moonlit amorphous carcasses. He made out deer and pig, and what could only be the quarters of a large wild bull. These cattle gone wild were the wariest creatures on the island, and this sign of the hunter's skill gave him another start of uneasiness. Backing off again on hands and knees, he cut himself a rabbit club of the right weight. Waiting for dawn, he whittled it, and bound with vine and a piece of shirt two sharp stones to the heavy end. He was skillful with it, and the feel of it in his hand was reassuring.

It was growing light.

THE BOAT APPEARED at sunup. Traver heard it a long way off, prowling the channel between islands at the southeast end. Now it drummed along the delta, just inside the bar, and headed straight in for the beach. It was a small, makeshift shrimp boat with rust streaks and scaling gray-green paint. Before it grounded, the hunter came out and, hoisting two small deer onto his shoulders, went down to the shore.

The two men loaded quickly. Then they stood a moment talking, the one on the pale sand of the beach, the other a black silhouette on the bow against the red fireball of the sun.

The boatman, who must have been in town the night

before, had probably confirmed whatever the hunter had noticed at the landing. Traver wondered if they would turn him in. He doubted it. In the prison denims, he could be shot on sight, and no questions asked—not that the hunter would require that excuse. He guessed that the latter had some right to be here, for otherwise, even in this lonely place, he would not occupy the cabin. He was probably a hired gamekeeper, poaching on the side. He would not want Traver here, and he would not want the sheriff nosing around the island either. He would want to take care of Traver by himself.

The man had come in and out of the cabin. He had the rifle in his hands, checking the action. His movements were calm and purposeful, and he gave Traver a good look at his face. It was a gaunt face, creased and hard, under heavy eyebrows, a shrewd face, curiously empty of emotion. Traver recognized that face, he had seen it all his life, throughout the South.

Ol' Redneck kill me, do he get the chance. And he mean to get the chance.

The man went off in the direction of Snake-house, moving swiftly into the trees.

For the moment, considering his situation, Traver stayed right where he was. He watched the shrimp boat disappear along the delta. His mouth was dry, and he licked dew from the grass. Though the early sun had begun to warm him, he felt tired and stiff and very hungry, and this hunger encouraged him to loot the cabin.

Unreal in the morning mist, the trees were still. The Spanish moss hung everywhere, like silence. The man would go to Snake-house, to the landing, to pick up Traver's trail, but it would not lead him far. Traver had stayed clear of the sand path, moving wherever possible on the needle ground beneath the pines. Still, if he meant to loot the cabin, he should hurry. And he was half-risen when a huge blue heron, sailing above the cedars into which the hunter had disappeared, flared off with a squawk and thrash of heavy wings.

Traver sank to his knees again, heart pounding.

That was close to bein you last worldly move. I mean, he layin fo' you, man, and he like to cotched you. I mean, he *smart,* doan you forget it, nigger. He know what you doin even fore you does it.

Traver waited again. When his heart stopped pounding, he began to laugh, a long quiet laugh that shook his big body like crying, and caused him to press his mouth to the crook of his arm. And he was surprised when tears came to his eyes, and the laughter became sobbing. He was frightened, he knew, and at the same time, he was unbearably excited.

You just a big black mule, you just a fool and a mule and a alligator all wrap into one.

He went on laughing, knowing his delight was dangerous, and all the more elated because of that. And as he laughed, he hummed to himself, in hunger.

Faraway and gone am I toward dat Judgment Day,
Faraway and gone am I, ain't no one gwine to stay,
Lay down dis haid, lay down dis load,
Gwine to take dat Heaven Road,
Faraway and gone am I toward dat Judgment Day.

In a while, far over toward the swamp, he heard the quack of startled black ducks, rising. When he saw their high circle over the trees, he got up on his haunches.

Could be dat a duck hawk, but most likely dat him. He over dar by Snake-house.

A string of ibis, drifting peacefully down the length of woods like bright white sheets of tissue, reassured him. Traver ran. In the open, he tensed for the rifle crack he could never have heard had it come, and zigzagged for the door. In less than a minute, he was back. He had a loaf of bread and matches, and was grinning wildly with excitement.

But now a fresh fear seized him. The hunter might return at any time, from any angle. If he did not hurry, he would no longer be able to maneuver without the terror of being seen. Traver stopped chewing, the stale bread dry in his mouth. Then he cut into the woods, loping in a low, bounding squat in the direction taken by the white man. At Graveyard-over-the-Bank, where once the cattle had been driven, penned, and slaughtered, he hid again. This place, a narrowing of the island, the man would sooner or later have to pass.

TRAVER STALKED HIM all that day. Toward noon, the hunter went back to the cabin. Traver could hear him rummage for the bread, and he wondered if, in taking it, he might only have endangered himself further by becoming, in the white man's eyes, more troublesome. The man came out again and sat on the doorsill, eating. His face, still calm, was tighter, meaner, Traver thought. The rifle lay across his knees. Then he rose and went away into the woods, heading southwest toward Cottonmouth Dike, and Traver followed.

The man made frequent forays from the path, but he seemed to know that he would not surprise his quarry, that

Traver was in all probability behind him, for though he moved stealthily out of habit, he made no real effort to conceal himself. Clearly, his plan was to lure Traver into a poor position, a narrow neck or sparsely wooded place where he might hope to turn and hunt him down. He set a series of ambushes, and now and then wheeled and doubled back along his trail. He was skillful and very quick, quick enough to frighten Traver, who several times was nearly trapped. Traver hung farther and farther behind, using his knowledge of the island to guess where the hunter would come and go, and never remaining directly behind, but quartering.

He was most afraid of the animals and birds, which, hunting and hunted, could betray his whereabouts at any time.

The white man was tireless, and this intensity frightened Traver, too. He seemed prepared to stalk forever, carrying his provisions in his pocket. When he ate, he did it in the open, pointedly, knowing that Traver could never relax enough to hunt, could only watch and starve.

By noon of the second day, Traver was desperate. When the man went west again, way over past Pig Root and Eagles Grave, Traver fled eastward to the landing and gorged on the coon oysters. Sated, he realized his mistake. He had a hundred yards of marsh to cross, back to the trees, and for all he knew, the hunter had doubled back again, and had a bead on him. He had done just what the man was waiting for him to do, he had lost the scent, and now any move he made might be the wrong one. He groaned at the thought of the vanished skiff—if only he'd gotten it ashore, and hidden it in the salt grass farther down. But now he was trapped, not only at the landing but on the island.

A bittern broke camouflage with a strangled squawk, causing Traver to spin around. In panic, he clambered up over the riverbank and ran back to the trees. The woods were silent. There came a faint cry of snow geese over the delta, and the sharp rattle of a kingfisher back in the slough. Downwind, wild cattle caught his scent and retreated noisily. Or was that the coming of the hunter? He pressed himself to the black earth, in aimless prayer. The silence grew, cut only by the wash of river wind in the old-field pine.

At dark, he fled into the marsh, and tried to rest in the reeds beneath a dike. Under the moon, much later, a raccoon picked its way along the bank, and he stunned it with his rabbit club. The coon played possum. When he crawled up to it, it whirled and bit him on the ankle. He struck it sharply with the stone end of the club, and it dragged itself into the reeds. He could not see it very well, and in a near frenzy of suppressed fear, he beat the dark shape savagely, long after it was dead. Panting, he sat and stared at the wet, matted mound of fur, the sharp teeth in the open, twisted mouth. He dared not light a fire with his stolen matches, and his gut was much too nervous to accept it raw. He left it where it lay and crept back to the woods and, in an agony of stealth, to Back-of-Ocean. He was overjoyed by the lamp in the cabin window.

He finally tuckered out, Traver told himself. The man done give ol' Traver up. Traver too spry for him.

The idea restored his confidence a little, and he chuckled without heart. He was still hungry, and he had no idea what his next move should be. Remembering the white man's face, he did not really believe he had given up the hunt, and this instinct was confirmed, at daybreak. The boat appeared again, and the white man met it, but he did not come out of the cabin. He stepped into the clearing from the yaupon on the other side. Traver had almost approached that way the night before. The light in the window had only been another trap.

Traver fought a wild desire to bolt. But he controlled himself, squeezing great fistfuls of earth between his fingers. He watched the hunter walk slowly to the beach and, resting his rifle butt on the silver roots of a hurricane tree, speak to the boatman. They were silent for a time, as if deciding something. Then the hunter shrugged, and shoved the boat from shore. It backed off with a grinding of worn gears. He returned to the cabin and came out of it a minute later. He had a cooked bone, and he pulled long strings of dry meat from it with his teeth. Traver stared at the lean yellow-brown of his face, the wrinkled neck, the faded khaki clothes and high cracked boots against the soft greens of the trees and the red cassina berries. He stared at the bone. The man tossed it out in front of him, then tramped it into the ground and lit a cigarette. Breathing smoke, he leaned against the cabin logs and gazed around the clearing. Traver caught the cigarette scent on the air, and stirred uncomfortably. The man flipped the butt into the air, and together they watched it burn away upon the ground. Then he shouldered the rifle and went back to the woods, and once more Traver followed.

Who huntin who heah? Traver tried to smile. Who huntin who?

The fear was deep in him now, like cold. He started at every snap and crackle and cry of bird, sniffing the air for scents, which could tell him nothing. There was only the stench of rotting vegetation, and the rank sweat of his fear.

He crept along closer and closer to the ground, terrified lest he lose contact with the hunter. In his heart, he knew there was but one course open to him. He could not leave the island, and he could not be killed. Both prospects were unimaginable. But he could kill.

Man, you in de swamp now. It you or him, dass all.

But he could not make himself accept this. He supposed he could kill a black man if he had to, and a white man could kill *him*. But a black man did not kill a white man.

Man, it doan matter what de color is, it just doan matter now. You in de swamp, and de swamp a different world. Dey ain't nobody left in dis heah world but you and him, and he figger dass too crowded. When ol' Lo'd passed out de mens's hearts, dis heah man hid behind de do'. A man like dis heah man, you let him run where he de law, and he kill you if you black or white or blue. He doan hate you and he doan feel sorry. You just a varmint dat got in de way, dass all.

But Traver doubted his own sense. Perhaps this man had nothing to hide, perhaps he was hunting legally, perhaps he would do no more than remove Traver from the island, or arrest him—how could he know that this man, given the chance, would shoot him down?

And yet he knew. He could smell it. He doubted his instinct because he hated what it told him, because he wanted to believe that this man also was afraid, that a man would not shoot another down without first calling out to him to surrender.

Man, he ain't called, and he know you heah. He quiet as de grave. And you take it in you haid to call you'self, you fixin to get a bullet fo' you answer.

AGAIN THAT MORNING, he was nearly ambushed. This time a rabbit gave the man away. For the first time, Traver lost his nerve entirely. He ran back east along the island and stole out on the marsh, crawling along the dike bank where he had killed the coon, persuading his pounding heart that food was his reason for coming. But he knew before he got there that the raccoon would be gone. Black vultures and an eagle rose in silence from the bank, and there was a flat track in the reeds where an alligator had come and gone, and there were blue crabs clinging upside down to the grass at the edge of the ditch. In the marsh, the weak and dead have a brief existence.

Traver was shifting his position when a bullet slapped into the mudbank by his head. Its whine he heard afterward, a swelling in his ears as he rolled into the water and clawed at the brittle stalks of cane across the ditch. A wind of teal wings, rising out of Dead Oak Pond, blurred his racket in the brake. He crossed a reedy flat and slid into a small pool twenty yards away. The echo of the shot diminished on the marsh, and silence settled, like a cloud across the sun.

Then fiddler crabs snapped faintly on the flat. Where he had passed, their yellow claws protruded, open, from the holes.

But he knew the man would come, and he tried to control the choked rasp of his breath. And the man came, picking his lean way along the dike, stopping to listen, coming on, as Traver himself had often done, tracking crippled ducks for the plantation gunners. Against the bright, high autumn sky, the hunter's silhouette was huge.

Traver slipped the rabbit club from his belt.

The man had stopped just short of where Traver had lain.

He squinted up and down the ditch. Though his face remained set, his right hand, wandering on the trigger guard and breech, betrayed his awareness that Traver might have a weapon.

He came a little farther, stopped again. He seemed on the point of calling out, but did not, as if afraid of intruding a human voice into this primeval silence. He bent and scratched his leg. Then, for a moment, scanning the far side of the dike, he turned his head.

Traver, straightening, tried to hurl the club, but it would not leave his hand. He ducked down and out of sight again. He told himself that the range had been too great, that the chance of a miss, however small, could not be taken. But he also knew he was desperate enough to have thrown it anyway, in agony, simply to bring an end to this suspense.

There was something else.

The man descended from the dike, on the far side. Almost immediately, he sank up to his knees, for there came a heavy, sucking sound as his boots pulled back. The man seemed to know that here, in the black resilience of the marsh, his quarry had him at a disadvantage, for he climbed back up onto the dike and took out a cigarette. This time, Traver thought he must call out, but he did not. Instead, he made his way back toward the woods.

Traver cursed him, close to tears. The hunter had only to watch from the trees at the end of the dike. Until dark, Traver was trapped. The hunter would sit down on a log and eat his food, while Traver lay in the cold pool and starved. The whole world was eating, hunting and eating and hunting again, in an endless cycle, while he starved. From where he lay, he could see a marsh hawk quartering wet meadows, and an eagle's patient silhouette in a dead tree. Swaying grass betrayed a prowling otter, and on a mud flat near him, two jack snipe probed for worms. Soon, in that stretch of ditch that he could see, a young alligator surfaced.

Thank de Lo'd it you what stole my coon. Thank de Lo'd dis pool too shaller fo' you daddy.

The alligator floated, facing him. Only its snout and eyes disturbed the surface, like tips of a submerged branch.

What you waitin on, Ugly? You waitin on ol' Traver, man, you got to get in line.

The insects had found Traver, and he smeared black mud on his face and hands. Northeast, a vulture circled slowly down on something else.

Whole world waitin on poor Traver. Whole world hangin round to eat on Traver.

And though he said this to cheer himself, and even chuckled, the sense of the surrounding marsh weighed down on him, the solitude. Inert, half-buried, Traver mourned a blues.

> Black river bottom, black river bottom
> Nigger sinkin down to dat black river bottom
> Ain't comin home no mo'
>
> Ol' Devil layin at dat black river bottom
> Black river bottom, black river bottom,
> Waitin fo' de nigger man los' on de river
> Dat ain't comin home no mo' . . .

At dark, inch by inch, circuitously, Traver came ashore. He knew now he must track the man and kill him. His nerves would not tolerate another day of fear, and he took courage from the recklessness of desperation.

Again the cabin was lit up, but this time he smelled coffee. The man's shadow moved against the window, and the light died out. The man would be sitting in the dark, rifle pointed at the open door.

The hunt ended early the next morning.

TRAVER BELLIED ACROSS a clearing and slid down a steep bank which joined the high ground to the marsh. His feet were planted in the water at the end of Red Gate Ditch, and on his right was a muddy, rooted grove of yaupon known as Hog Crawl. The hunter was some distance to the eastward.

Traver had a length of dry, dead branch. He broke it sharply on his knee. The snap rang through the morning trees, and a hog grunted from somewhere in the Crawl. Then Traver waited, peering through the grass. He had his knife out, and his rabbit club. Lifting one foot from the water of the ditch, he kicked a foothold in the bank. Below him, the scum of algae closed its broken surface, leaving no trace of where the foot had been.

The man was coming. Traver could feel him, somewhere behind the black trunks of the trees. The final sun, which filtered through the woods from the ocean side, formed a strange red haze in the shrouds of Spanish moss.

Out of this the man appeared. One moment there was nothing and the next he was there, startling the eye like a copperhead camouflaged in fallen leaves. He moved toward Traver until he reached the middle of the clearing, just out of Traver's range, facing the Hog Crawl. There he stood stiff as a deer and listened.

Traver listened too, absorbing every detail of the scene through every sense. The trap was his, he was the hunter now, on his own ground. The cardinal song had never seemed so liquid, the foliage so green, the smell of earth so strong.

The white man shifted, stepping a little closer. The hog snuffled again, back in the yaupon. Traver could just make it out beneath the branches, a brown-and-yellow brindle sow, caked with dry mud. Now it came forward, curious. It would see Traver before it saw the white man, and it would give him away.

Traver swallowed. The sow came toward him, red-eyed. The white man, immobile, waited for it also. When the sow saw Traver, it stopped, then backed away a little, then grunted and trotted off.

Traver flicked his gaze back to the man.

He was suspicious. Slowly the rifle swung around until it was pointed a few feet to Traver's left.

He gwine kill me now. Even do I pray, O Lo'd, he gwine kill me now.

Traver was backing down the bank as the man moved forward. Beneath the turned-down brim, the eyes were fixed on the spot to Traver's left. Traver flipped the butt of broken branch in the same direction. When the white man whirled upon the sound, Traver reared and hurled his club. He did not miss. It struck just as the shot went off.

Traver had rolled aside instinctively, but this same instinct drove him to his feet again and forward. The man lay still beside the rifle. The hand that had been groping for it fell back as Traver sprang. He pressed his knife blade to the white, unsunburned patch of throat beneath the grizzled chin.

Kill him. Kill him now.

But he did not. Gasping, he stared down at the face a foot

from his. It was bleeding badly from the temple but was otherwise unchanged. Pinning the man's arms with his knees, he pushed the eyelids open with his free hand. The eyes regarded him, unblinking, like the eyes of a wounded hawk.

"Wa'nt quite slick enough fo' Traver, was you!" Traver panted. He roared hysterically in his relief, his laughter booming in the quiet grove. "You fall fo' de oldes' trick dey is, dass how smart you is, white folks!" He roared again into the silence. "Ol' Traver toss de branch, ol' white boy fooled, ol' white boy cotch it in de haid! I mean! De oldes' trick dey is!"

Traver glared down at him, triumphant. The man lay silent.

Traver ran the knife blade back and forth across the throat, leaving a thin red line. He forced his anger, disturbed by how swiftly his relief replaced it.

"You de one dat's scairt now, ain't you? Try to kill dis nigger what never done you harm! You doan know who you foolin with, white trash, you foolin with a man what's mule and gator all wrap into one! And he gone kill you, what you think 'bout dat?"

The man watched him.

"Ain't you nothing to say fore I kills you? You gone pray? Or is I done killed you already?" Uneasy astride the body of the white man, Traver rose to a squat and pricked him with his knife tip. "Doan you play possum with me, now! You ain't foolin me no mo', I gone kill you, man, you heah me?"

For the first time, Traver heard his own voice in the silence, and it startled him. He glanced around. The sun was bright red over the live oak trees, but quiet hung across the marsh like mist. Out of the corner of his eye, he watched the white man with suspicion, but the other did not stir.

He dead, Traver thought, alarmed. I done killed him dead.

Avoiding the unblinking eyes, he picked up the rifle and stared at it, then he laid it like a burial fetish back into the grass. Now he stepped back, knife in hand, and prodded the body with his toe.

"Git up, now!" he cried, startling himself again. "You ain't bad hurt, Cap'n, you just kinda dizzy, dass all. Us'ns is got to do some talkin, heah me now?"

But the body was still. A trail of saliva dribbled from the narrow mouth, and a fly lit on the grass near the bloody temple. Traver bent and crossed the arms upon the narrow chest.

"You fall fo' de oldes' trick in de world," Traver mourned, and shook his head. "Dass what you done." Badly frightened, he talked to comfort himself, glancing furtively around the clearing.

He started to back away, then bolted.

The man rolled over and up onto his knees, the rifle snatched toward his shoulder. He sighted without haste and fired. Then he reached for his hat and put it on, and turned the brim down all around.

Then he got up.

Traver was a powerful man and did not fall. He could still hear the echo and the clamor in the marsh, and he could not accept what was happening to him. He had never really believed it possible, and he did not believe it now. He dropped the knife and staggered, frowning, as the man walked toward him. The second bullet knocked him over backwards, down the bank, and when he came to rest, his head lay under water.

His instinct told him to wriggle a little further, to crawl away into the reeds. He could not move. He died.

1957

THE
WOLVES
OF
AGUILA

On those rare occasions when a lean gray wolf wandered north across the border from the Espuela Mountains, trotting swiftly and purposefully into the Animas Valley or the Chiricahuas or Red Rock Canyon as so many had in years gone by, describing a half-circle seventy miles or more back into Mexico, and leaving somewhere along its run a mangled sheep or mutilated heifer, then Miller was sent for and Miller would go. He was a wolf hunter, hiring himself out on contract to ranchers and government agencies, and if the killing for which he was paid was confined more and more to coyotes and bobcats, the purpose of his life remained the wolf. He considered the lesser animals unworthy of his experience, deserving no better than the strychnine and the cyanide guns that filled the trunk of his sedan. Even the sedan had been forced upon him, when the wolf runs which once traced the border regions of New Mexico and Arizona had become so few and faded as to no longer justify the maintenance of a saddle pony. The southerly withdrawal of the gray wolf into the brown, dust-misted mountains of Chihuahua and Sonora had come to Will Miller as a loss, a reaction he had never anticipated. He was uneasily aware that persecution of the wolf was no longer justified, that each random kill he now effected contributed to the death of a wild place and a way of life that he knew was all he had.

Nevertheless, with mixed feelings of elation and penitence, he would travel to the scene of the last raid. There he would scout the area for scent posts where the wolf had left fresh sign. Kneeling on a piece of calf hide, he worked his clean steel traps into the earth with ritualistic care, rearranging every stick and pebble when he had finished, and carrying off the displaced dirt on the hide. His hands were gloved and his soles were smeared with the dung of the livestock using the range, and leaving the scene, he moved away backward, scratching out his slightest print with a frayed stick. Nor did he visit his traps until the wolf had time to come again, gauging this according to the freshness of the sign and according to his instinct.

Because of his silence and solitary habits, his glinting eyes and wind-eroded visage, his full Navajo blood, Miller was credited with the ability to think like an animal. His success was a border legend, and while it was true that he understood its creatures very well, he was successful because he did not take their ancient traits for granted. The dark history of *Canis lupus,* the great gray wolf of the world, he considered an important part of his practical education. Not that Miller accepted the old tales of werewolves and wolf-children, or not, at least, in the forefront of his mind. But the heritage in him of the Old People, the deep-running responses to the natural signs and sacraments, did not discount them. The eerie intelligence of this night animal, its tirelessness and odd ability to vanish, had awed him more than once, and he had even imagined, in his long solitude, that should he ever pursue it into the brown haze to the south, the wolf spirit would revenge itself in that shadowed land. Such knowledge lent his life a mystery and meaning that the church missions could not replace, and his mind asked no more. He was not a modern Indian, and he shunned the modern towns. Like the wolf itself, he abided by older laws.

NIGHT POWERS WERE incarnate in the Aguila wolf, which was known to have slaughtered sixty-five sheep in a single night and laid waste the stock in western Arizona for eight long years, fading back into the oblivion of time in 1924. One trapper in pursuit of it had disappeared without a trace, and Miller had always wondered if, at some point in that man's last terrible day beneath the sun, the Aguila wolf had not passed nearby, pausing in its ceaseless round to scent the dry, man-tainted air before padding on about its age-old business. Somewhere its progeny still hunted, and he often thought that the black male that once circled his traps for thirteen months and dragged the one that finally caught it forty miles must have descended from the old Aguila.

Most wolves gave him little trouble. Within a week or ten days of its raid, the usual animal would trot north out of Mexico again and, retracing its hunting route in a counterclockwise direction, investigate the scent posts, pausing at each to void itself and scratch the earth. At one of these, sooner or later, it would place its paw in a slight depression, the dirt would give way, and the steel jaws would snap on its foreleg. If its own bone was too heavy to gnaw through, and the trap well staked, it would finally lie down and wait. It would sense Miller's coming and, if still strong enough, would stand. Though its hair would bristle, it rarely snarled. Invariably, Miller stood respectfully at a distance, as if trying to see in the animal's flat gaze the secret of his own fascination. Then he would dispatch it carefully with a .38 revolver. But when the wolf lay inert at his feet, a hush seemed to fall in the mesquite and paloverde, as if the bright early-morning desert had died with the shot. The red sun, rising up, would whiten, and the faint smell of desert flowers fade, and the cactus wrens would still. In the carcass, already shrunken, lay the death of this land as it once was, and in the vast silence a reproach. The last time, Miller had broken his trap and sworn that he would never kill a wolf again.

Some years passed before two animals, hunting together according to the reports, made kills all along the border, from Hidalgo County in New Mexico to Cochise and Santa Cruz counties in Arizona, with scattered raids as far west as Sonoita, in Sonora. They used the ancient runs and developed new ones, but their wide range and unpredictable behavior had defeated all efforts at trapping them. The ranchers complained to the federal agencies, which in turn sent for Will Miller.

Miller at first refused to go. But he had read of the two wolves, and his restlessness overcame him. A few days later, he turned up in the regional wildlife office, a small, dark, well-made man of forty-eight in sweated khakis, with a green neckerchief and worn boots and a battered black felt hat held in both hands. Beneath a lank hood of ebony hair, his hawk face, hard and creased, was pleasant, and his step and manner quiet, unobtrusive. He had all his possessions with him. These included eight hundred dollars, a change of clothes, and the equipment of his profession in the sedan outside, as well as an indifferent education, a war medal, and the knowledge that, until this moment, he had never done anything in his life that had dishonored him. Placing his hat on the game agent's desk, he picked restlessly through the reports. Then he asked questions. Angry with himself for being there, he hardly listened while the agent explained that the two wolves seemed immune to ordinary methods, which was why Will had been sent for. Miller ignored the patronizing use of the Indian's first name as well as the compliment. Unsmiling, he asked if the two wolves were really so destructive that they couldn't be left alone. The agent answered that Miller sounded scared of *Canis lupus* after all these years and, because Miller's expression made him uneasy, laughed too loudly.

"Them wolves was here before we come," Miller said. "I'd like to know they was a few left when we go."

Miller went west to Ajo, where he got drunk and visited a woman and, before the evening was out, got drunk all over again. He was not an habitual drinker, and drank heavily only in the rueful certainty that he would be sick for days to come. Later he drove out into the desert and staggered among the huge shapes of the saguaros, shouting.

"I'm comin after you, goddam you, I'm comin, you hear that?"

And he shook his fist toward the distant mountains of Mexico. In doing so, he lost his balance and sat down hard, cutting his outstretched hand on a leaf of yucca. Glaring at the blood, black in the moonlight, he began to laugh. But a little later, awed and sobered by the hostile silhouettes of the desert night, he licked at the black patterns traced upon his hand and shivered. Then he lay down flat upon his back and stared at the eternity of stars.

Toward dawn, closing his eyes at last, he sighed, and wondered if it could really be that he felt like crying. He jeered at himself instead. Unable to admit to loneliness, he told himself it was time he settled down, had children. He could decide who and how and where first thing in the morning. But a few hours later, getting up, he felt too sick to consider the idea. He cursed himself briefly and sincerely and headed south toward Sonoita, where the wolves had been reported last.

The town of Sonoita lies just across the border from the organ-pipe cactus country of southern Arizona, on the road to Puerto Peñasco and the Gulf of California. Miller arrived there at mid-morning. The heat was searing, even for this land, as menacing in its still might as violent weather elsewhere. The Mexican border guards were apathetic, waving him through from beneath the shelter of their shed.

Miller had a headache from the alcohol and desert glare. Making inquiries, he found no one who understood him. Finally, by dint of repeating *"Lobo, lobo"* into the round, rapt faces, he was led ceremonially to the parched remains of a steer outside the town. The carcass had been scavenged by the people, and a moping vulture flopped clumsily into the air. The trail was cold. Since Sonoita lay on the edge of the Gran Desierto, he did not believe that the wolves would wander farther west. From here, he would have to work back east, to New Mexico, if necessary.

Yet the villagers picked insistently at his shoulder—*Sst! Señor, sst!*—and pointed westward. When he stared at them, then shook his head and pointed east, they murmured humbly among themselves, but one old man again extended a bony, implacable arm toward the desert. Like children, mouths slack, hands diffident behind their backs, the rest surrounded Miller, their black eyes bright as those of reptiles. *Sí, amigo. Sí, sí.* They gravitated closer, not quite touching. *Sí, sí.* Abruptly, he pushed through them and returned into the town.

Clutching a beer glass in the cantina, encircled by his silent following, he knew he had not made a thorough search for wolf sign, and could not do so in his present state of mind. The prospect of long days ahead in the dry canyons, piecing out the faded trail, oppressed him so that he sat stupefied. He felt sick and uneasy and, in some way he could not define, afraid. He wanted to talk to someone, to flee from his forebodings, and he thought of a nice woman he knew in Yuma. But Yuma lay westward a hundred miles or more, via an old road across the mountain deserts to San Luis and Mexicali. He did not know the road, and he had heard tales of the violence of this desert, and he dreaded the journey through an unfamiliar land in his present condition, and in such heat. On the other hand, these people had directed him toward the west. How could they know? Considering this, he felt dizzy and his palms grew damp. Still, by way of San Luis, he could reach Yuma by midafternoon and come back, in better spirits, tomorrow morning. Meanwhile, the wolves might kill again in Sonoita, leaving fresh sign. And if he got drunk enough, he thought, he might even come back married.

"To hell with it," he told the nodding Mexicans. "I'll go."

Outside, the heat struck him full in the face, stopping him short. His lungs squeezed the dry air for sustenance, and his nose pinched tight on the fine mist of alkali shrouding the town. In the shade, the natives and their animals squatted mute, awaiting the distant rains of summer. The town was inert, silent, in its dull awareness of Miller's car.

At the garage, Miller checked his oil and water carefully, knowing he should carry spare water with him, for the San Luis Road, stretching away into the Gran Desierto, would be long and barren. But he could not locate a container of any kind, and his growing apprehension irritated him, and on impulse he left without the water, quitting the town in a swirl of dust and gravel. Once on the road, however, he felt foolish, and he was not out of sight of the last adobe hut when he caught himself glancing at the oil pressure and water temperature gauges. He did it again a few minutes later.

THE ROAD RAN WEST through low, scorched hills before curving south into the open desert. At one point it ran north to Quitobaquito Springs, the only green place on the San Luis Road. Miller stopped the car. Across the springs, beneath a cottonwood, he saw a hut; a family of Papagos, two dogs, and a wild-maned horse gazed at him, motionless. The dogs were silent. In the treetops, two black, shiny phainopeplas fluttered briefly and were still.

"How do," Miller called. The Indians observed him, unblinking. It occurred to Miller that his was the only voice in this dead land, where people answered him, when they answered at all, with nods and grunts and soft, indecipherable hisses. He stood a moment, unwilling to think, then returned slowly to the sedan.

For a mile or so beyond the springs, a gravel road detoured from a stretch of highway left long ago in half-repair. The detour was rutted and pocked with holes, and he could barely keep the toiling car in motion. He was easing it painfully onto the highway again when he heard a clear, animal cry. The sound was wild and shrill, and startled Miller. Braking the sedan, he stalled it. In the sudden silence, the cry was repeated, and a moment later he glimpsed a movement at the mouth of a hollow in a road bank. An animal the size of a large dog slipped from the hole. In the glare, he did not recognize it as a child until it stood and approached the car. This creature, a boy of indefinite age, was followed instantly by another, who paused on all fours at the cave entrance before joining the first.

Already the first was at the window, fixing Miller with clear, flat eyes located high and to the side of his narrow face. His brother—for their features were almost identical—had brown hair rather than black, and his eyes were dull, reflecting everything and seeing nothing. Over the other's shoulder, he looked past Miller rather than at him, and after a moment turned his head away, as if scenting the air. Then the first boy smiled, a reflexive smile that traveled straight back along his jaw instead of curling, and pointed his finger toward the west. When he lowered his hand, he placed it on the door handle.

Miller could not make himself speak. He stared at the hole from which the two had crept, unable to believe they had really come out of it, unable to imagine what they were doing here at all. His first thought had been that these boys must belong to the Papago family at the springs, but one look at their faces told him this could not be so. These heads were sharp and clear-featured, reminiscent of something he could not recall, with a certain hardness about the mouth and nostrils. There was none of the blunt impassivity of the Papagos. There was nothing of poverty about them, either, and yet clearly they were homeless, without belongings of any kind. Still, they might be bandit children. He peered once again into the black eyes at the window, but his efforts to remember where he had seen that gaze were unsuccessful, and he shook his head to clear his dizziness.

The boys watched him without expression. After a while, when he did nothing, the older one opened the door and slipped into the car, and the second followed.

Miller felt oddly under duress. Moving the car forward onto the highway, he glanced uneasily at the gauges. It upset him that the Indians had not inquired as to where he was going. On the San Luis Road, one came and one went, but one made certain of a destination. It was as if, were he to drive his car off southward across the hard desert into oblivion, those two would accompany him with fore-knowledge and without surprise.

At last he said, in his poor Spanish: *"En donde va? A San Luis? Mexicali?"*

The older boy smiled his curious smile and nodded, hissing briefly between white teeth. Miller took this to mean *"Sí."*

"San Luis?" Miller said.

The boy nodded.

"Mexicali?" Miller said, after a moment.

The boy nodded. Either he did not understand, or the matter was of no importance to him. He raised his hand in a grotesque salute and smiled again. The eyes of the other boy switched back and forth, observing their expressions.

Though the heat had grown, the day had darkened, and odd clouds, wild scudding blots of gray, swept up across the sallow sky from the remote Gulf. A wind came, fitfully at first, fanning sand across the highway. Miller, in a sort of trance, clung to the wheel. His car, which he knew he was driving too fast, was straining in the heat, and he sighed in the intensity of his relief when a large orange truck, the first sign of life in miles of thinning mesquite and saguaro, came at him out of the bleached distances ahead.

He glanced at the two boys. They seemed to have sensed the coming of the truck long before Miller himself, for their eyes were fixed upon it, and the eyebrows of the elder were raised, alert.

As the truck neared, an arm protruded from the cab and flagged Miller to a stop.

The truck driver, lighting a brown cigarette, peered about him at the hostile desert before speaking, as if sharing the desolation with Miller. He then asked in Spanish the distance to Sonoita. Miller, who was now counting every mile of the hundred-odd to San Luis, knew the exact distance, and suspected the truck driver knew it, too. The chance meeting on the highway was, for both of them, a respite, a source of nourishment for the journey which, like the springs at Quitobaquito, was not to be passed up lightly. However, he could not think of the correct Spanish numeral, and when the other repeated the question, inclining his head slightly to peer past Miller at the Indians, Miller turned to them for help. Both boys stared straight ahead

81

through the windshield. The Mexican driver repeated the question in what Miller took to be an Indian dialect, but still the boys sat mute. The older maintained his tense, alert expression, as if on the point of sudden movement.

"Treinta-cinco," Miller said at last, choosing an approximate round figure.

The driver thanked him, glancing once again at the two boys. He exchanged a look with Miller, then shrugged, forcing his machine into gear as he did so. The truck moaned away down the empty road, and the outside world it represented became a fleeting speck of orange in the rearview mirror. When Miller could see it no longer, and the solitude closed around him, he inspected his temperature gauge once again. The red needle, which had climbed while the car was idling, returned slowly to a position just over normal, flickered, and was still.

The road ran on among gravel ridges, which mounted endlessly and sloped away to nothing. Only stunted saguaros survived in this country, their ribs protruded with desiccation, and an abandoned hawk's nest testified to the fact that life had somehow been sustained here. Miller, who had seen no sign of wildlife since leaving the springs, wondered why a swift creature like a hawk would linger in such a place when far less formidable terrains awaited it elsewhere. And of course it had not remained. The nest might be many years old, as Miller knew, and the hawk young, mummified, might still be in it. On this sere, stifled valley floor, a crude dwelling, forsaken and untended, would remain intact for decades, with only dry wind to eat at it, grain by grain. Not, he thought, that any man could survive here, or even the Mexican wolf. And he had convinced himself of this when, at a long bend in the road, an outcropping of rock he had seen from some miles away was transformed by the muted glare into a low building of adobe and gray wood.

Removing his foot from the accelerator, he wiped his forehead with the back of a cold hand. The black sedan, still in gear, whined down across a gravel flat of dead saguaros.

The cantina lay fetched up against a ridge just off the highway, as if uprooted elsewhere and set down again, like tumbleweed, by some ill wind. Around it the heat rose and fell in shimmers; he thought it abandoned until he saw the hot glitter of a trash heap to one side. There were no cars or horses. Beside him, the older boy stared straight ahead, but he gave Miller the feeling that his vision encompassed the cantina, on one side, and Miller himself on the other. Both boys were pressed so close to the far window that there was a space between them and Miller on the narrow seat, and a tension as tight as heat filled the small compartment. Miller opened his door abruptly and got out. When the two turned to watch him, he pointed at the cantina and waited. After a moment, the dark boy reached across the younger one to the door handle, and both slipped out on the far side.

By the doorway, Miller paused and touched a hide stretched inside out upon the wall, allowing the Indians to draw near him and trail him into the cantina. He could not put away his dread, and the idea of leaving them alone with the car and equipment made him uneasy. But although they had moved forward, the two boys paused when he paused, like stalking animals. Heads partly averted, squinting in the violent sun of noon, they followed his hand upon the pelt, as if his smallest move might have its meaning for them. For a moment, indecisive, he inspected the sun-cracked skin, through the old wounds of which the grizzled hair protruded. The wolf had been nailed long ago against the wall, and although most of the nails had fallen away, it maintained its tortured shape on the parched wood. With the tar paper and tin, the hide now served to patch the shack's loose structure. One flank and shoulder shifted in the wind from the Gran Desierto, and the claws of the right forefoot, still intact, stirred restlessly, a small, insistent scratching which Miller stifled by bending the claws into the slats. In doing so, he freed a final nail, and the upper quarter of the hide sagged outward from the wall, revealing the scraggy fur. Miller stooped to retrieve the nail. Half-bent, he stopped, then straightened, glancing back at the mute boys. Their narrow eyes shone flat, unblinking. He turned and moved through the doorless opening, stumbling on the sill.

In a room kept dark against the glare, a man sat in a canvas chair behind the bar. He stared blindly at the sour walls, as if permanently ready to do business but unwilling to solicit it. The only sound was a raw, discordant clanging of a loose tin sheet upon the roof, the only movement dust in the bright doorway. For a moment, Miller imagined him carved of wood, but at the tip of a brown cigarette stub in the center of his mouth was a small glow.

"Buenos días," he said.

The proprietor's answer was a soft tentative whispering, scarcely audible above the clanging of the tin. Asking for a beer, Miller whispered, too. In answer, the man reached behind him into a black vat of water, drawing out a bottle with no label. He held it at arm's length like a trophy, the stale water sliding down his wrist. The vat, roiled by his hand, gave off a fetid odor.

"All right," said Miller. *"Sí."*

He turned to locate the two boys. The older one stood outside the doorway, but the other was not in sight. Miller waved at the first to enter, but the boy did not stir. The proprietor, glimpsing him for the first time, glanced at Miller. Miller took the tepid beer and requested two bottles of soda. The man held up two fingers, raised his eyebrows. "There's another outside," Miller explained. He awaited the warm bottles, then walked quickly to the door.

The younger boy was squatted beneath the pelt, staring away over the desert. Though his head did not move, his eye flickered once or twice, aware of Miller, who sensed that, should he make a sudden motion, this creature would spring sideways and away, coming to rest, still watching him, after a single bound. Wild as they were, however, the two seemed less afraid of him than intent upon him. He could not rid himself of the notion that these wild, strange boys had been awaiting him in their cave near the Quitobaquito Springs.

The dark boy drew near and took the two bottles of soda from Miller's hands. The exchange was ceremonial, without communication. The squatting boy, in turn, received his bottle from the other, clutching it with both hands and sniffing it over before bending his head and sucking the liquid upward.

Miller returned inside to get his beer, and leaned backward heavily against the counter. His headache had grown worse, and the smell of the rancid water on the bottle sickened him. He put it down, seizing the counter as a wave of vertigo shrouded his sight, and the boy in the doorway wavered in black silhouette.

From somewhere near at hand, a soft voice probed for

his attention. He recovered himself, sweating unnaturally, heart pounding.

"*Lobo* . . ."

"Yes," he heard his own voice say, "that's a fine wolf hide . . ."

". . . *el lobo de Aguila* . . ."

"No," Miller murmured. "*No es posible.*"

"*Sí, sí,*" hissed the proprietor. "*Sí, sí.*"

"No," Miller repeated. He made his way to a crate against the wall and sagged down upon it, clasping his damp hands in a violent effort to squeeze out thought.

"*Sí, amigo. El lobo de Aguila* . . ."

Wind shook the hut, and spurts of sand scraped at the outside wall. Miller heard the crack of stiffened skin as the wolf hide fell. He pitched to his feet in time to see it skitter across the yard toward the open desert, in time to see the squatting boy run it down in one swift bound. He crouched on it, eyeing Miller over his left shoulder, the hair on the back of his head erect in the hot wind. At Miller's approach, he backed away a little distance, not quite cringing. Miller took the hide to the proprietor, who peered at all of them out of the shadows. The dark boy, when Miller glanced at him, smiled his wide, sudden smile.

The water in his radiator was still boiling when he removed the cap. He refilled the radiator with liquid from the beer vat inside, aware of the tremor in his hand. Paying the man, he dropped the money to the ground and had to grope for it. The two boys moved toward the car in response to some signal between them, and the man in the doorway, clutching the hide, hissed for Miller's attention.

"*Señor* . . ."

He did not continue, and would not meet Miller's eyes.

"Adiós," Miller said, after a moment, and the man's lips moved, but no whisper came.

The motor, still hot, was hard to start, and the car, once moving, handled sluggishly. Miller rolled the windows up to close out the gusts of heat, but after a moment he could not catch his breath. Gasping, he rolled them down again. The two boys watched him.

According to his reckoning they were now halfway to San Luis. In early afternoon, the temperature had risen and the glare, oddly bright beneath an intermittent sun, was painful to his eyes. He saw with difficulty. His passengers seemed not to mind the heat, absorbed as they were with his expressions, the movements of his hands.

Miller's intuitions ran headlong through his mind, but a curious despair, a resignation, muted them. He would reach San Luis or he would not, and that was all.

THE SEDAN WAS passing south of the Cabeza Prieta Mountains, great tumbled barrens looming up out of the foothills to the northward. Somewhere up there, Miller had heard, lay the still body of a flier, who only last week had left a note in his grounded plane and wandered west in search of help. He had not been found. In this weather, in this desert, a man made a single mistake, a single, small mistake—say, a mislaid hat, a neglected landmark, an unfilled canteen . . . He must have expressed part of this thought aloud, for the dark boy was nodding warily. When Miller squinted at him, he smiled.

"You wouldn't last six hours out there," Miller told him. "Don't matter *who* you are."

The boy nodded, smiling.

Miller laughed harshly, and the second boy sat forward

on the edge of his seat, eyes wide. Abruptly, Miller stopped and turned away. He felt lightheaded, a little drunk.

THE LANDSCAPE ALTERED quickly now, and mountains appeared in scattered formations to the south. Their color was burnt black rather than brown, and their outlines looked crusted. Farther on, they crowded toward the road, extending weird shapes in heaps of squat, black boulders. The dull gravel of the desert floor was invaded, then replaced, by sand, and the last stunted saguaros disappeared. With every mile, the sand increased in volume, overflowing the rock and creeping up the dead crevasses. The huge boulders sank down, one by one, beneath bare dunes, until finally the distances were white, scarred here and there with outcroppings of darkness. On the road itself, broad tongues of sand seeped out from the south side, and the sky turned to a sick, whitish pall, like the smoke of subterranean fires.

They had entered the Gran Desierto. He thought about the mountains of the moon.

Miller looked a last time at his gauges. The oil pressure was stable still, but the temperature needle, a streak of bright red in the monotone of his vision, was climbing. He knew he should slow the whining car, but he could not. Huddled together, his passengers sat rigid, eyes narrowed to slits against the sea of white. The younger one was panting audibly.

Miller tried to talk, but no sound came. The dark boy gazed at Miller, then placed his arm about his brother's shoulder.

A tire split before the water went, and the car swerved onto the sand shoulder of the road. He wrenched at the wheel in a spasm of shock, and the sedan lurched free again

like a mired animal, stalling and coming to rest as the rear
tire settled. Miller fought for breath. He sat a moment
blinking, as the sand, in wind-whipped sheets, whitened the
pavement. Then he got out, and the two boys followed.
Retreating a little distance, they observed him as he opened
the trunk and yanked the jack and lug wrench and spare tire
from the litter of bags and traps.

The cement was too hot to touch, and the unseen sun too
high in the pale sky to afford shade. Miller spread his
bedroll and kneeled on it, working feverishly but ineffec-
tually. He felt near to fainting, and the blown sand seared
his face, and he burned his hands over and over on the hot
shell of the sedan. But he managed at last to free the tire,
and was fighting the spare into place when a sound behind
him made him whirl. The dark boy stood over him, holding
the iron lug wrench.

Miller leapt up, stumbling backward.

"Christ!" his voice croaked. Crouching, he came forward again, stalking the child, who dropped the wrench and
moved away. Miller picked it up and followed him. The
younger was squatting on the roadside, lifting one scorched
foot and then the other, and emitting a queer, mournful
whine. His brother took his hand and pulled him away.
Unwilling to leave the shelter of the car, they kept just out
of reach. When Miller stopped, they stopped also, peering
uneasily at the wrench in his clenched hand. Then Miller
raised the wrench and went for them, and the younger
moaned and ran. The older did not move. Miller, lowering
his arm, stopped short. The boy's gaze was bared, implacable. Then he, too, turned and moved after the other, and
took his hand. Miller watched until their small shimmering
forms disappeared behind black boulders.

89

Swaying on the road, Miller licked his lips. Something had passed. Maybe the kid was only trying to help, he thought. What the hell's the matter? Didn't you see them children holding hands?

"You ignorant bastard," he murmured, stunned. He repeated it, then cried aloud in pain. He ran to the car and finished the job, leaving the tools and broken tire on the road. The motor started weakly, but in his desperate efforts to turn the car around, he sank it inexorably into the sand of the road shoulder. The engine block cracked and the car died. He got out and stared. Then he started off, half-running, in the direction taken by the children.

Nearing the boulders, he stopped and shouted, *"Niños, niños!* I don't mean no harm!"

But his throat was parched and his tongue dry, and the sound he made was cracked and muted. Somewhere the boys were taking shelter, but if they heard him, they were afraid and silent. Over his head, the sun glowed like a great white coal, dull with the ash of its own burning, without light.

"Niños!"

He knew that if he did not find them, they might die. Tired, he entered the maze of rocks, calling out every little while to the vast silence. The rocks climbed gradually in growing masses toward a far black butte, and as the day burned to its end, the wind died and a pallid sun shone through the haze. It sank away, and its last light crept slowly toward the summit, reddening the stones to fierce magnificence, only to fade at sunset into the towering sky.

Miller toiled up through the shadows. He reached the crest toward evening, on his knees, and his movement ceased. From somewhere below, a little later, he heard a

shrill, clear call, and the call was answered, as he awoke, from a point nearer. In the dream, the children had walked toward him hand in hand.

He sat up a little, blinking, and fingered the dry furrows of his throat. To the north, the flier's empty eyes stared up, uncomprehending. But Miller, without thinking, understood. His hand fell, and as his wait began, his still face grew entranced, impassive. The rocks turned cold. About him, in strange shapes of night, the mountains of Mexico gaped, crowded, leapt and stretched away across the moonlit wastes. The nameless range where he now lay stalked south through the Gran Desierto, sinking at last on the dead, salt shores of the Gulf of California.

1958

HORSE
LATITUDES

Our ship—a British freighter that hauled Christmas trees and small machinery from New York Harbor down through the Antilles to South America and up the Amazon—had scarcely left Pier B in Red Hook when an amusing fight broke out between the occupants of one of her two cabins. Since it was I who occupied the other (at the behest of the travel associations, I was composing a brochure on freighter travel), and I liked things to myself, I had no wish to alter our arrangements, nor was I—I'll be candid—in the least anxious that these natural enemies escape each other, since the forty-day voyage that lay ahead promised little enough in the way of entertainment.

Horace, shrill with good cheer in the Lord, was a Baptist missionary returning to his glum flock in the jungle. The morose Hassid, a Lebanese merchant who shrugged constantly, resignedly, in awareness of the whole world's weight on his soft shoulders, was impelled by a sallow destiny toward Belém, at the river's mouth, where customs required that he appear in person with his wares—television sets and small refrigerators, together with two gigantic outboard motors. Hassid was fluent in four languages, having traveled widely in the world—the sure mark of a fly-by-night in the eyes of Horace, who had traveled scarcely anywhere beyond Mato Grosso and east Tennessee. In response to the missionary's brash inquiries regarding his religious affiliations, "if any," Hassid mentioned a Protestant grandmother, a Freemason father, and a lingering acquaintance with the Church in Rome. Horace referred to this suspicious figure as "the Turk," making it a point never to use his name, while Hassid used his tormentor's name at every opportunity, deeming this sufficiently insulting.

The Baptist was a sprightly boyish sort with a snap-on pink bow tie. For hours at a time he hunched over his new shortwave radio, "awaiting orders from on High," his roommate said, although all he was doing, I'd discovered, was crooning accompaniment to the latest tunes from Finland and Cambodia.

"Enjoys music," I assured Hassid. "He's quite harmless."

"He is very harmful to me," Hassid snarled.

These cabin mates' one common bond had placed them instantly in competition, and our first meal was a sorrowful affair. Just recently the Lebanese had suffered the removal of an abscess from his nose, which he stroked continuously, his moist brown eyes appealing for commiseration. The missionary, not to be outdone, described in detail to the table—where sat at that moment, in addition to ourselves, the First Mate and the Chief Engineer, observing the new passengers in some alarm—the even more recent excision of some pesky hemorrhoids, a triumph over the Forces of Darkness for which he gave full credit to the Lord. Horace had an odd squawking voice and a sudden shrieking laugh perhaps more pleasing to the Antichrist than to his Maker. Uttered now for no apparent reason, it confounded the poor Levantine, who took his slighted nose into both of his soft hands and peered through his ringed fingers at his shipmate.

"What is it you call yourself?" the Turk hissed finally. "Horse ass?"

"Hor-ace," said Horace. "An upright Christian name."

"With a *W?*" Hassid inquired archly, directing this question to me. He winked just to bedevil Horace, knowing the missionary would not acknowledge such a joke even if he got it. From that point on, as the friend of these two enemies, I served them as both referee and foil, tossing in small provocations just to keep things lively.

"Turk," mused Horace, chewing carefully.

"Whore-ass," Hassid murmured here and there during the meal, shaking his head in gloomy wonderment, while the two Britons huddled over their food.

OUR SHIP SAILED OUT that evening into North Atlantic storms, and by next day Hassid's soiled complexion had turned sickly. Propped up at the mess table, he looked embalmed. At the noon meal, Horace informed him that he looked "poorly," at which Hassid put his whole face in his hands. "I been noticin them li'l beads of sweat on yo' upper lip," Horace continued, just before Hassid bolted from the table. "Smell that fish?"

Horace complained about the fish smell in the galley. He

could not bear the sight or smell of fish. The Lord ate fish, I reminded him, stirring things up to rally Hassid, who was losing their struggle by default, but Horace put me nicely in my place.

"He probably liked it," Horace said, and Hassid had the ingratitude to smile.

The Turk did his best to appear at meals, since the Chief had told him that food was the best cure for seasickness. The long days of rough seas had "knocked us back a bit," in the Chief's phrase. The slow pace exasperated Hassid when he was well enough to feel emotion, since he'd already missed a swifter ship owing to the operation on his nose. If he got "indisposed" even once again, he'd quit this ship of fools at the next port and fly to Belém.

"How to kill this time?" Hassid begged each day, rolling his soft eyes heavenward in supplication. "How to kill this time?" He was the only man I ever knew who tore his hair—I thought this habit had gone out of fashion. In fair weather, he crouched up in the bow, staring away toward southern destinies, in hope of nothing. The Chief responded to his ceaseless plaints by saying that a man had best be patient about arriving anywhere. "What is a day, a week, even a month, after all?" he once inquired—an old, sad, touching observation that the Turk misconstrued in his great misery as an affront.

The Chief was an amiable old Scot, gone bald and a bit bleary with hard use. Though scarcely garrulous, he doubtless was considered so by the First Mate, whom we never saw except across the table. The First was a rufous, blocky man who detested anything not known in Liverpool, but happily he talked little while he dined. Having stuffed his gob with thick bread gobbets until his soup was set before

95

him, he proceeded doggedly through the little menu, taking all choices in the order listed, plate after plate, like somebody packing a bag. The one dish he would not consume was "American mutton," a weekly entrée which lent our menu its one hint of international cuisine. (I asked him once what distinguished "American" mutton. "Different animal altogether," huffed the First.)

In Bermuda, our first port of call, Horace passed the day at a small white table in an ice-cream parlor, writing sappy postcards to his wife and drinking soft, sweet drinks. Hassid sat with him, head in hands, in an ennui that would persist another fortnight, all the way, in fact, to Port-au-Prince. "Got your sea legs yet?" Horace would ask him every little while, and wink at me. I suggested reading as a cure, but the Turk's sole interests were young girls and commerce. Reading, he said, made him nervous, and as it happened, a dislike of books was the one thing he and Horace would agree upon. Despite their enmity, he had acquired a taste for Horace's company, having doubtless perceived that his dark dream of undoing this man's moral superiority was all that stood between him and his monstrous boredom. For his part, the missionary clung to some fond hope of redeeming the sybaritic Turk, whom he preached to nightly.

And so, to amuse myself, I set one upon the other, confident that both secretly enjoyed this. "Their claws," as someone once remarked of a somewhat more auspicious pair, "were set so deep into each other that if they pulled apart, they would soon bleed to death."

BOUND FOR HAITI, our freighter trailed smoke south through the horse latitudes, where in other times dead horses were heaved overboard from ships becalmed in the

Sargasso Sea. Horace, still cheerful to a fault, had held the upper hand on the bounding main of the North Atlantic, but in the pewter calms of the horse latitudes his companion began to stir into dull life, and ashore in Haiti, where seasickness no longer stayed him, Hassid moved very quickly to the fore. Scarcely had his slippered foot touched land—and land, moreover, where his favorite tongue was the official language—when he stood full-blown before us, a true *bon vivant* whose delicate French and urbane manner made him the natural leader of our little party. Who then if not the bold Turk dismissed Port-au-Prince as unworthy of our custom? No, no, quoth he, we would hire a conveyance and escape the sea, *à la campagne, à la montagne*! So enchanted was he by this inland prospect that he waved his arms in fine Gallic abandon, inadvertently inciting to near hysteria the hordes of jobless Haitians who rushed along with us, desperate to attend to every need.

The human din, the forceful smells, the ribald colors of the waterfront juxtaposed with grinding poverty and filth, drove Horace to condemn the Roman Church, which he blamed—with bitter looks at Hassid—for the plight of this beautiful, unhappy country. Politically oblivious, Hassid ignored him, having commenced dealings with a sober-suited native who had persevered so with his winks and hisses as to commend himself at last to the Turk's attention. Even now our new Haitian acquaintance was revealing the existence of another friend, almost as dear to him as we were, who knew more about Haiti than anyone since Toussaint l'Ouverture. As luck would have it, this same friend was the master of a splendid car designed perfectly for whatever purpose *les gentilshommes* might have in mind. This friend, said he, might be engaged upon short notice, and sure enough, a spavined Ford came forward even as he spoke, honking and backfiring along the curb. Its clairvoyant chauffeur turned out to be none other than Charles (*"Tous mes amis Americains m'appellent Shar-lie"*), the international authority on Haiti, who swore he would place his awesome expertise at our disposal for a *prix d'ami* that was nothing short of laughable. In proof of this he laughed, more or less merrily, hurling his car door wide to show us in.

Gold-toothed and fragrant in a many-colored shirt, Charlie was as festive as Pierre was somber, and his black skin shone in the very places where Pierre's old hide looked gray and dull. Adjusting his tone from the first instant to the whims of Hassid, he said, Yes! Yes! We would make a *tour de ville,* and afterward *un petit séjour à la campagne, à la montagne*—and afterward? Here Charlie permitted himself a discreet pause, an elevation of the eyebrow, recognized at once by the worldly Turk, who fetched poor Horace a whack across the back. It now transpired that Charlie's rate had been set so ludicrously low owing to his confidence that *après?* . . . his new friends would refresh themselves at a private *club* of his acquaintance where nice clean girls of eighteen were awaiting us.

"Cloob?" Horace whimpered.

"Maison de rendezvous!" Hassid exulted, embarking at once on a spirited discussion of what lay in store for us. "They don't call you Whore-ass for nothing!" he told the missionary—for my benefit, since Horace would never in a month of Sundays understand this subtle *jeu de mot*.

"Well, this boy's not ronday-vooin at no durn *cloob,*" Horace hollered. "Gonna ronday-voo right back to that durn *boat*!"

Fearful—as I thought at first—of losing his advantage, the Turk assured the highly agitated missionary that this talk of cloobs meant nothing whatsoever. "I suppose I'm used to folks who speak the truth," said Horace, with a sniff of pinch-nosed sanctimoniousness that collapsed Hassid in silent harem mirth. He had not seen Horace wink at me.

Negotiations concluded, we set off in Charlie's car, accompanied by the glum Pierre, who wished to keep an eye on his investment. Honking his way up the main street, our guide stopped at every shop to extol its ethnic wares. Only Horace bought a few peculiar odds and ends, to perk up his mission in Brazil, and Charlie's repute must have suffered in these places. Relieved to whisk us from the city, he drove off in a scattering of dogs and children for Pétionville, up in the mountains.

At a quaint hostelry decked in poinsettias, Charlie disappeared into the kitchen, hoping we would decide to eat while we awaited him. He did not bother his head about Pierre, who perched his cadaverous frame on a kind of dunce's stool just by the doorway, the better to watch our consumption of lean steak and local greens. Even the hard heart of Hassid was touched by Pierre's mournful demeanor, but our offer of sustenance was declined with dignity. He required no food for himself, Pierre intoned, but if we wished, he would accept a monetary offering with which he might hope to feed his hungry children.

Charlie emerged, wiping his mouth, and we drove on. Burping a little, he discoursed freely on the subject of the ex-slave Dessalines, as well as on Pétion, Henri Christophe, Toussaint l'Ouverture—"Dat is my hero *à moi*," said Charlie, pointing at himself—and other champions of Haitian independence. Not infrequently during our journey,

99

this enterprising man with the gold incisor would shout *pow-pow-pow!* in wild patriotic fervor, to demonstrate how the Haitians of old shot down the French. Why modern Haitians did not do as much for their modern despots he would not say.

From atop a mountain, we gazed down upon Port-au-Prince and the great Gulf of Gonave, assailed the while by five musicians who stepped from a bush to coax hideous sounds from hollow gourds and other unpromising implements. Our freighter, loading a cargo of grain meal across the bay, was a mere white speck in the blue distance. At a shop which enjoyed our guide's unqualified approval, the curios, though more costly, were otherwise identical to those in Port-au-Prince—sisal and mahogany, real voodoo fetishes, real voodoo drums conveniently inscribed "Souvenir of Haiti," stuffed hawksbill turtles, crafted seashells, and other useful Caribbean gewgaws. The whole display was enshrined on film by Horace, who made the tortuous journey down the mountain more exciting by shouting at Charlie to stop on each blind turn so that he might "snap" the bright-clothed native women, the fruit baskets and flower-bedecked burros, swaying down against the sky and distant sea.

SINCE CHARLIE had flattered us as *types sportifs,* we permitted him to transport us to the cockfights, which were held on Saturdays and Sundays in a rickety arena on the city's outskirts. The vivid plumage of cock and man was intensified that afternoon by the tropic sun that came pouring like gold air through the slats as through a stained-glass window—or so, at least, I read aloud to Hassid from what I was writing on the "local color" page in my field notebook. Horace, diverted momentarily from the fights, the bets, the reek of cane liquor, the wicked happy laughs of "fallen women," denounced my irreligious simile in no uncertain terms as he changed film.

"Should a missionary witness such things?" Hassid asked Horace. "Blood sports and gambling? Scarlet women?"

"Lord Jesus did," Horace informed him, adjusting his pink bow tie.

The cocks, shorn of combs and tail plumes, were rangy little roosters of starved and hard-bitten demeanor. Prior to the fight, their leg horns, or spurs, had been rasped to two sharp points, and water was now spat copiously upon them, lest they expire of heat prostration before winning money for their owners. For the first suspenseful moments, the two birds circled, beak to beak and taut as arrows. Then the doomed things jumped and fluttered, pecked and spurred until one dropped. The loser never learned from hard experience but went right on flailing at the stronger bird. When finally it toppled from exhaustion and loss of blood, the victor, itself close to death, squatted down and blinked.

Feeling ran high at the cockfight, each telling coup greeted with stamps and hoots, or loud cries of *Bis, bis!*— Again, again!—and another round of reckless betting. Between fights, the bird owners crowded pell-mell into the tiny ring, insulting one another at the top of their lungs as if to invigorate their charges. The cocks, which were wedged beneath their arms, facing backward, missed no chance to go at each other *en passant*.

The crowd of sinners made a glorious spectacle.

"Most of these poor lost souls are your feller Catholics," Horace told Hassid, not bothering to come out from behind his camera. "We'll title this one 'Sodom and Gomorrah.' " 101

"You seem to be enjoying this as much as they are," Hassid nagged Horace.

"Have mercy, Lord"—*click*—"they know not what they do."

"I hate you," Hassid said, with sudden feeling.

"Forgiveness is divine," said Horace. "I forgive you."

From the cockfights we repaired once more into the countryside, to the coastal villages and bright green rice paddies along the southern shore of La Gonave. The haunted appearance of thin country folk, the strangled graveyards on the silver bay, made me ask Charlie if any real voodoo was still practiced. After some muttering about "way back in de mountain," Charlie changed the subject, not because I had struck a hidden vein of native folkways but because he had been distracted from his purpose, which very shortly came to light.

Without warning, he ran the old Ford off into a rutted side road, nearly killing an old woman who was trying to cross. Ignoring Horace's frantic queries, he drove up smartly to a villa on the shore where a large group of lightly clad young ladies (members of the *cloob,* I assured Horace) were taking the air of afternoon under the palms.

"Drive on! Drive on!" cried Horace, gaze averted.

I assured him that there were colors, shapes, and sizes for even the most spiritual taste, all wearing the most angelic smiles imaginable. A few now rose and sashayed forward, as Hassid flared his nostrils in anticipation. "Whore-ass, you have come to the right place," he gloated, poking the forefinger of one hand through the fist of the other.

"Drive on!" Horace implored him. *"Please.* Drive on!"

Just then, a girlish voice rose above the dulcet clamor. "Hey, Joe!" the siren called, "I yam a virgin!"—an unpardonable insult to the Turk's intelligence, it appeared, since he immediately frowned and turned away. Yet what he had heeded, I realized later, was the anguished yelp of a soul about to be cast down into perdition—was it that, or was it Horace's use of his first name?

"Please, Hassid," Horace had whispered, leaning forward and pressing his brow to the back of the front seat.

Hassid stared straight ahead and did not speak. Then, shrugging his shoulders in apology, he asked me gently, "All right, my friend? What is a day, a week, a month, after all . . . ?" And to our astonishment, he folded his arms on his chest and sat back with a lordly sigh.

"Drive on," he said.

Poor Pierre, half-turned in the front seat, shook his bony skull in unashamed grief. Failing to avail ourselves of these young women, his expression said, might prove a mortal blow to his poor children. As for Charlie, he gave vent to his outrage in a furious burst of speed that nearly wrecked his car in the deep ruts. Pursued by a large and savage dog—nowhere to be seen as we drove up—we hastened away to the coast road and the harbor, our entire sojourn having occupied less than a minute.

Horace, by his own fervent statement, had never had carnal knowledge of a woman other than her to whom he had cleaved in holy matrimony. To his dismay, the wicked Turk, regretting, perhaps, his kindly gesture, spoke lightly of a carnal caper in the morgue. These revelations, which came to light in the high excitement that followed our departure from the private club, engaged our attention all the way back to the ship.

Under hard lights, in the steaming air, soft sacks of meal tumbled by stevedores raised a fine dust from the freighter's

103

hold. The day aboard ship, the Chief confided, had been uneventful save for one thrilling event: The First, intoxicated, had attempted to descend a rope boarding-ladder without troubling to secure it properly beforehand, and had descended farther than he might have wished, into the bay.

Dominica, Saint Lucia, Barbados, Saint Vincent, Grenada, Trinidad. Horace no longer went ashore except to mail letters to his wife and pay calls on the local missionaries. He had produced a thin mustache which did not suit him, and a pair of shorts which suited him still less, and perhaps these accoutrements dissuaded his peers from offering him the opportunity to preach that his heart desired. The nearer he drew to wife and children, the more he gave way to abject homesickness. Try as we would to tease him out of it by promising him young girls at Port of Spain, he did not rise up to denounce us, as he once had, but only complained dispiritedly of the smell of fish, which had escaped its unknown source and trailed him everywhere. And still he wrote daily to his wife, even when our journey was so advanced that no letter would reach her before he did.

"*What* do you tell?" Hassid would yell, tearing his hair. "Excuse me, I don't get it! You reveal how many pieces of meat you ate up at your dinner, or what is it? What happened to you on this stinking ship between yesterday and now? What can you possibly be *saying* to her? *What?*"

"You would know that, Hassid, if you'd ever found a wife," Horace said pityingly. He winked at me, but Hassid did too. I felt an unexpected twinge of isolation.

We left the Windwards in our wake, cleared Port of Spain. Day after day, down the long and empty coast of the wild continent, the freighter rolled southeastward through an olive sea, against the might of the equatorial current. The long meals were purgatorial, the white sun mute; the cargo gave off a sweet reek, the warm air thickened. Once again Hassid was seasick and depressed, and took such comfort as he could from reviling Horace. In the iron bow, hands fluttering like birds, they shrieked their love song to the wind, stick figures lifted toward the far light of heaven, plummeting again, on the oily clouds of the vast tropic horizon.

1959

MIDNIGHT
TURNING
GRAY

Once, when approaching the hospital
by the side road through the woods, she knew she would
round the final bend to find it gone—not gone, precisely,
but sunk back into that coarse New England hillside like
a great crushed anthill, its denizens so many mad black dots
darting in and out and over the dead earth. Earlier she had
imagined that the season here was always autumn, and she
struggled still with an idea that the inmates, in some essential way, did not exist at all.

But Lime Rock State Mental Hospital surged out from
behind the corner of the wood, awaiting her. Her heart
quickened: if the sun shines here, she thought irrationally,
it must shine everywhere.

She was relieved to see the buildings. There were always
figures on the woods road, figures whose status or intent

was never certain. And patients, as one of the nurses had once warned her, tried now and then to get away. In her caution, Anne Pryor perceived in all strange faces on the grounds a certain secretive sly sickness, and was glad each morning of the protection of the buildings, where the ill, organized like livestock, were dealt with by the duly authorized.

The wings of each building extended toward the recesses of others, in a pattern like a puzzle pulled apart, and unless one knew one's way—as Anne, though three weeks here, was certain she did not—the puzzle seemed malevolent and confusing. The roofs of these buildings were slate and steep, overhanging dark grilled porches set into the ends, like caves, and the windows, hollow-eyed and barred, crouched back in brick of a rufous earthen color. This color pervaded the place, even to the lifeless ground from which it rose.

For though Lime Rock Hospital had stood for thirty years, it had never been absorbed by the countryside. Rather than creep forward to camouflage its outline, the growth on this New England hill had seemed to shrink away, leaving it more and more exposed. The grass was thin, and the earth maintained its excavated look. It had a violent iron smell, like blood.

This morning the smell was muted by the new November cold. Leaving the car in the yard behind the Administration Building, Anne took a last deep breath before entering its basement by the fire door. In the converted boiler room Dr. Sobel and Mrs. McKittredge and Harry Marvin were having coffee. Dr. Sobel put down his cup as Anne entered the room and said good morning to her as he left. Every day Dr. Sobel, an odd soft little man with a Phi Beta Kappa key, moved a little more quickly, more intensely, toward the wards. He called them the Augean Stables. The term was facetious, and Dr. Sobel was not a facetious man. He used it only because he did not want people to tell him—as Mrs. McKittredge, or Mac, as she was called, had long since told him—that, for his own sake, he ought to recognize the element of hopelessness in his task.

"He's going to die here, old Doc Sobel, and he may be a patient by the time he does." Harry Marvin, twenty-eight, was sallow and dark, with a long cropped head and a manner which was not Harvard, as he imagined, but only faintly effeminate. He had been, in the war, a pharmacist's mate, and on this slim medical background based his opinion, shared by Anne, six years his junior, that she had neither the experience nor the temperament to work here.

"Mental hospitals," Mac remarked, "must settle for what they can get." In saying this, she implied no criticism of Dr. Sobel but was simply stating for the first time that day her favorite fact. Mac was a social worker and, unlike Sobel, was less concerned with the patients than with their treatment at the hands of the state. "And what do they get?" she demanded. "They get the Sobels, who are too starry-eyed to see that two thirds of what their salaries should be go for the mushrooms on those politicians' steaks. They get the Harry Marvins, whose medical training wouldn't qualify them for a job in an Old Dogs' Home. And they fill in with little student nurses and nice kids like Anne, who are overworked for nothing!"

"Well, they have *you* anyway, Mac," Anne said, her tentative laugh defeating the remark.

"That's true," Mac said, and grinned obligingly. Between her fingers a permanent cigarette, goaded by a mannish thumb, flicked up and down like the tail of a nervous bird.

"I've got to get over to the Monkey House," Harry Marvin said. Harry worked in the children's wards and, like Dr. Sobel, had given his task a name. Anne had once thought that the term referred to the usual clamor of children, or that it bore, perhaps, a cute-as-monkeys context. But on her first visit there, her senses explained it far more harshly. And its aptness breached a strict staff code by which all inmates were thought of, and referred to, as "patients," though the majority were beyond all aid and went untreated, even by Dr. Sobel.

Mac's wry wrinkled face winced openly at that name, but she said nothing. She was a practical woman, and clearly she knew that Harry Marvin did his work and, however flippant, did it very well. Nevertheless Mac disapproved. She seemed to sense a danger that Anne, too, had recognized already—that if, even for one moment, they were to acknowledge the degradation of their charges, to regard them openly as unworthy of respect and love, to regard them as subhuman, if once, in short, they succumbed to uneasy laughter, then all pretense would disappear, and the hospital would no longer be a hospital but a prison.

Harry Marvin knew this, too. Glancing at them, he frowned, discomfited. "Well, I'm off," he said, after a moment. "You, too, Anne?"

"She hasn't had her coffee," Mac rebuked him.

"No, I don't need it, Mac." Anne's tone of breathless apology, abetted by a startled, mournful look, was characteristic of her manner. Inviting protection, it drew people to her, yet she felt at times that she spoke too loudly, even bumptiously, and was conscious of a certain coarseness in her stance and gait more becoming, her mother had told her pointedly, to a tall boy of thirteen. Though pretty in an impermanent way, she had not yet learned to show herself to best advantage.

Or so said Harry Marvin, the very first time she had spoken with him alone. Shyly, she had sought him out because he was her generation and might supply the friendship essential to her in this place. But Harry had no time for frivolity. His was the clinical approach, and during their second talk, he made a number of observations on her sexual patterns, or rather, the absence of them. Disguised in his white frock, his fingertips together, he had lured her into admission of inexperience. As a cure he prescribed his own caress, and when she refused it without quite meaning to, accused her of being neurotic. His astonishment suggested that any girl resisting him might well end her days as a patient in Lime Rock State Mental Hospital. He went on to discuss her appetites, sublimated, he assured her, because as an only child she needed to dominate her widowed mother. Anne sought for the missing link in his diagnosis, which seemed a rash *non sequitur* and was, besides, inaccurate. Her mother, poor but proud, clung to her good family name and had never been dominated by anybody. But Anne, embarrassed by his use of the word "appetites," nodded meekly in agreement. Too insecure to spy insecurity in another, she was anxious only to change the subject.

Anne and Harry walked in silence up the stairs and out the front door and along the driveway toward Anne's building. The driveway continued down the slope to the front gate, which hid in the maple trees off the highway. So as to draw less attention to the hospital and its unwelcome presence in the township, the staff and the rare visitors were encouraged to use the back road through the woods. The precaution seemed foolish, since the mass of raw structures, like a glacial deposit on its hillside, was a landmark for miles around. Yet its approaches were obscure, there were few signs. Though bald and exposed on its terrain of broken, rocky fields, the hospital, as one came nearer, sank out of sight into the woods.

"I suppose Mac took offense at my reference to the Monkey House." They had paused at the door of Anne's occupational therapy unit, which formed part of the ground floor of one of the buildings.

"Oh, I don't think so. She knows you were only joking."

"Listen, if you don't want to get like Sobel, you have to relax once in a while, that's all. And the Monkey House is the most depressing ward in the place. I mean, you always *hope* in there, and you're always disappointed. So many of those kids are basically sound, or would be if only—"

"I know!" Anne said. "Have you met Ernest Hamlin?"

Interrupted, Harry shook his head in irritation. "Who's Ernest?" he said.

"Oh, he's a patient. He comes to O.T. now. But I mean, he's basically sound. I've *talked* to him," Anne offered as proof, speaking faster and faster. "He says—"

"Maybe they all are," Harry said, and turned his back on her.

"Ernest Hamlin really is, though," Anne called after him.

She watched him go, then turned and entered the outside door, unhappy. The inner door required a key, and she paused to hunt for it in her purse. As usual, she was very nervous, and today, upset by Harry Marvin, she dropped the key upon the floor.

On her first visit to the occupational therapy unit—and

111

surely this unit was the least threatening in all of Lime Rock, since only patients in control of themselves were allowed here without special supervision—she had felt a revulsion based on fear which passed immediately to vertigo and nausea. She had had to sit down, perspiring and cold. It had frightened her, that revulsion, since it was so baseless. There was nothing fearsome about the patients at O.T. Perhaps if they hadn't gazed at her in that wide-eyed way, perhaps if the ward hadn't smelled of children, of crude clay bowls and varnish, paint, of balsa wood and cardboard games, of apples and faint urine in the makeshift clothes . . .

Thus she was grateful for Ernest Hamlin.

Ernest had come the previous Tuesday at the hour of the weekly square dance, which was for Anne the most upsetting occasion of her week. Though eliciting a forlorn gaiety in the patients, it was grotesque in its laughter without merriment, in the heavy aimless prancing, in the pairing off of illness and of age. Here a wan old woman clutched a dreaming black man; there a smiling student nurse propped up a bashful moron. Beyond, a lank-haired catatonic in a knee-length twenties frock performed wild stumbling pirouettes all by herself. Along the walls the others watched, despairing, giggling, excited by the din, some clapping vaguely out of time with the piano.

"Don't you want to dance?" Anne cried.

"No, thank you, miss," said a big fair boyish man poised for escape by the door to the room where some played shuffleboard, and for a moment Anne imagined him a visitor.

"I haven't seen you here before," she ventured. He faced her then and smiled.

"Oh, I'm a patient all right, miss," he said.

"I see," she said and, ineffectual, flushed. "My name is Anne."

"Mine's Ernest Hamlin." He enclosed her outstretched hand in his. "I come down to do something with my hands"—he held them out and gazed at them—"so's I wouldn't go nuts." He smiled again at her involuntary start, then sat down carefully on the edge of a folding chair.

She seated herself beside him.

"I ain't really nuts, you see, miss, not yet, anyways." He glanced pointedly at the dancers. "I guess these poor dopes claim that quite a lot."

"Nobody here is really 'nuts,' Mr. Hamlin," she blurted dutifully. "They only—"

"You know what I mean, Miss," Ernest told her. "Mentally ill. I ain't really mentally ill, not yet, anyways." Again he observed the dancers, wincing. "I'll make the grade, though, one of these fine days."

"You mustn't feel sorry for yourself," Anne said. "You mustn't—"

"No?" he said. His heavy face turned to her once again. It was an intelligent face, rueful, perceptive, alight with quiet humor, quite different from the gallery of faces in the room. He was not yet dead in the way that people died here, their hair first, then the mouth and eyes, all but the hands. At Lime Rock the hands, like infants' hands, or those of the old man frozen in his chair beside them, clung to life, whether clenched or groping. "No, maybe I shouldn't," Ernest said and, frowning, changed the subject.

"Do most of these folks know why they're here?" he said.

"The ones aware of anything do. They don't believe it, most of them." She waited for him.

"Oh, I *believe* it, all right," he told her quickly. "There

113

ain't no doubt about what *I* got. I got a piece of shrapnel sitting too close in to my brain to operate, understand? They can't operate. And every once in a while this shrapnel sort of acts up, like, and drives me nuts with pain—mentally ill with pain," he corrected himself. "I get so's I don't know what I'm doing even. I get destructive. I'm supposed to be dangerous, miss, because I don't know what's going on. So this vets hospital, they give up on that piece of shrapnel after a while, they classify me a mental case, they got no provisions for guys like me, they send me here. I didn't even get no chance to go on home and see my folks, or the boys in my shop, or nothing. And I got a mother waiting home, and sisters, and I got a part interest in this machine shop home. I'm a machinist." He gazed at his hands again, big useful hands sitting idle on his knees. "A damn good one, too," he muttered angrily. "I worked for them there at the hospital sometimes, and the guy running the shop, the super there, he said he never seen better work." He shook his head. "Which is why I come down here this afternoon, I thought maybe you had some tools and stuff, a lathe, maybe, but there ain't nothing here but shuffleboard, and knitting needles, and games for kids."

She nodded, mute.

"So that's about it: they sent me up here, and I ain't mentally ill. My fiancée wrote me a letter already. She said it would be better to make a clean break. She said it hurt her worse'n it did me." Ernest Hamlin almost smiled. "But I'm just a young guy, I got a long life ahead of me, and guess where it looks like I'm going to spend it—" He stopped short, as if shocked anew by the realization. "Jesus," he whispered, "I can't believe it."

114   He set back gently upon her feet a fat, loose-lipped girl

in baggy dungarees who had square-danced into him and fallen. The girl put her hands on her hips and swaggered with gross coyness away from him. Her dancing partner was a scraggy female who carried her head shot forward like a turkey and seemed on the point of tears.

"So I feel sorry for myself," he concluded.

Anne nodded, overcome.

He cocked his head, alert to her emotion. "I didn't want to trouble you, miss. You were just being nice listening to all that stuff, doing your job. A lot of the staff around here are pretty tough," he added.

"They have to be tough," Anne said. "That doesn't mean that they're not nice."

"Yeah, I guess that's right. Like this guy they got in charge of the disturbed ward. This guy is out of this world. I mean, they put *me* in there at first, with all them foul balls. Maybe you ain't never seen that ward. They got about fifteen nuts in there, the dangerous ones, except they ain't dangerous all the time, not most of them. He's got some beauties in there, this guy.

"The first day he takes me by the arm, like a priest or something, and he says, 'C'mon, Ernest, I want you to meet the boys.' The boys are sitting around a table shelling peas, all but one. 'That's Phil,' the guy says. 'Phil's a nice fellow, but he bites. You let Phil get his teeth into you, and you're in trouble. He has to be *pried* off. So you'd better keep a little distance when you talk to Phil.' This Phil is sitting in the corner making a lot of racket, moaning and grunting and all. I didn't feel much like talking to him, then or later, although I *did* give it a whirl one day. Some conversation! I don't think he *could* talk, if you want to know the truth, he was in pretty bad shape. I mean, he *looked* bad, like some

115

loony in the movies or something, like the way I thought they *all* looked here before I come. Anyway, this superintendent or whatever you call him, *he* chats with Phil all the time. You'd think they was buddies from way back. And he talks to them other birds the same way. The others don't look as bad as Phil, they can mostly talk and all. They gave me the creeps, though.

"When I was introduced, I said, 'Hi, boys.' Not a peep out of them, not one of them. They all just watch me, sitting at the table with them peas. The super acts like everything is hunky-dory. 'Pull up a chair,' he says to me, 'and get acquainted.' Then one of these guys picks up a pea and rolls it across the table at me. I catch it as it goes over the edge. 'Thanks a lot, Bill,' I says—I'd caught his name, see—and I eat the goddam pea. This Bill flashes me a kind of smile. Then another guy starts hollering that I'm eating up all his peas, he wants to know why he's shelling in the first place, he pays his taxes, don't he, he ain't no lousy kitchen help. So this Bill gives me a big wink and knocks the other guy's bowl of peas into his lap and all over the floor. Just like that. And winks again. He *likes* me, see. And this other guy—I expected all hell to break loose, but it didn't—this other guy, he gets down on his knees and picks up all his peas one by one, and when he comes up for air he's grinning. Not really grinning, but watching this Bill in kind of a crafty way, like, and humming and nodding his head, and you could tell he was going to fix Bill for keeps, later on, he had it all figured out, only he never did. And then—listen, do you want to hear about all this, or do you want me to shut up?"

"No, please go on, Mr. Hamlin. I've never been in that ward, it's interesting."

116

"Yeah, it is." Ernest was pleased. "It's interesting. But I appreciate you listening. I ain't had much chance to talk to nobody I could talk to. I talked some to that super, though. What a guy. He spoke to me like I was the only one in there who could understand. That's the way he talked to all of them, even Phil—as if they were the only normal ones in the outfit. I don't know what he said to the others about me. He probably said, 'Watch out for that goddam Ernest, boys, he's mentally ill, he'll break your back as quick as look at you!' "

Ernest burst out laughing, and the sound rose high and loud against the clamor of feet and music and broken voices. Anne stared at him, dismayed. He was laughing so violently that in the animal closeness of the room he had to loosen his collar. But now he coughed and stopped, as quickly as he had started. "No," he murmured, "I ain't the kind to hurt nobody if I can help it. Even in Korea, I didn't like it." He sat there for a moment in silence, then got to his feet. "Goodbye," he said, and went through the door of the shuffleboard room before she could think to call him back.

When he appeared the following afternoon, Anne felt unaccountably relieved. He wore a tie this time, of a deep green cheap material which bulged and twisted the collar of his denim shirt. Though the tie flew in her honor, he did not approach until he saw she was unoccupied. Then he came immediately and said, "I been thinking about what you told me, about how I hadn't ought to feel sorry for myself—"

And she wanted to say, Oh, I didn't mean it, I was talking foolishly, you have every right . . .

"—and that's true, what you said, but I still do." He was

117

clearly ashamed but continued doggedly, as if making a compulsory address. "Why I feel sorry is, I'm so damned useless. I can't *do* nothing, even for somebody else. I just got to sit here until I rot!"

"No, listen, Mr. Hamlin—"

"Jesus, call me Ernie, will you, Anne!" he cried, throwing his big hands into the air in a gesture of pain. Sheepish, he followed her to a seat at the side of the room.

"Listen, Ernie, maybe you can help us here. The staff needs help, it's much too small. Look, I'm in O.T. with one nurse today, and two wards coming in. We can't handle everybody properly. If you could—"

"Sure, sure, I know. I already talked to that super in the disturbed ward, before he got me transferred. I asked him if there wasn't something around for me to do, and he said, no, they couldn't pay me nothing, there wasn't enough salary to go around as it was. Can you beat that? For a job like that, locked up twelve months a year with those foul balls? Knowing they might jump him every time he turns his back? And that ain't why he's nice to them, either, he's just nice, that guy, and he's got guts!" Ernie, excited in his admiration, had forgotten momentarily about himself. "If I ever get out of here, I'm going to talk to somebody about that pay he gets! He ain't complaining, but he says himself he wouldn't do it only he's leery what kind of a creep would replace him for that kind of money. So he keeps on doing it, year after lousy year!"

Anne nodded, watching him. He was pounding his fist into his palm, beside himself. After a moment, she murmured, "Ernie, I wasn't thinking about a salaried job. I just thought you might be interested in helping out when you felt like it. It would keep you busy, and be a real contribution."

"Oh, sure. I mean, I'd be glad to help, Anne. I was thinking about a *job,* though, maybe outside, mowing lawns or something. That way, if I got a little money I could send it home. That way, I could kid myself I was helping to support my mother or something, see?" He turned to her, his big face pale. "Because another thing I figured out last night was that the best thing that could happen to me if I'm going to have to stay in this place"— and his tone suggested that he had yet to face this fact—"is that I go nuts. I mean, really honest-to-God mentally ill. Then maybe I won't care no more, and get a big bang out of square dancing with all my buddies."

"Ernie, please listen."

He shook his head, masochistic now, determined to have it out with himself. "It wouldn't be so hard," he muttered. "If people ain't nuts when they come in to this place, they sure as hell must be by the time they get out. You can't keep company like this and not have some of it rub off." He nodded bitterly at an old woman across the room who was remarking at the top of her voice upon the fact that staff members had no right to occupy themselves with just one patient, when other patients such as herself needed their pillows straightened behind their heads. "See that," he said. "She knows I like to talk to you, need to talk to you just to keep from going under, and she's going to do her best to pull me down there with the rest of them. Well, she'll make it yet."

"This isn't like you," Anne said, thinking to shame him. She knew her concern was partly selfish, since his self-control, and the companionship it guaranteed, were essential to her as well.

"No, it isn't," Ernie admitted. He glanced at her, as if to inquire how she knew. "I guess it's because you're kind

119

of a doctor, like." He frowned. "You ain't, though, right? You're just a kid trying to help these people. Well, you're helping me, whether you know it or not." He blushed and stood up. "Forget, it, okay, Anne? I ain't going to bother you no more."

"You haven't bothered me," Anne told him truthfully. "I like to talk to you."

"Sure, sure." He had his back to her, hands in pockets. "So what do you want me to do to help you out?" he said, after a moment. "Shall I break that old woman's neck?"

They laughed together, disheartened.

"Just talk to people, Ernie. Help me talk to people. I run out of words after a while."

"I ought to be good at that. I never run out of words in my life, as I guess you found out." He grimaced, dismissing her protest with a gesture of his hand. "Okay. What'll I talk to them about?"

"Ernie," she said.

He paused, then turned to her, waiting.

"Look, you mustn't feel badly about telling me everything," she started. "If I were in your shoes, they'd have to drag me around screaming."

Still he waited.

"Only I guess you'll have to make the best of it. I hope you'll talk to me whenever you want." As always when she was ill at ease, she talked faster and faster. "And I admire your courage, and I'm going to try to help you."

"Help me?"

"Yes. I don't think you belong in here. I think it's unfair," Anne said, and regretted the impulse, afraid. "There probably isn't much I can do." She backed down before his breathless gaze, which hardened, then softened again. He

120

was gentle enough to pretend she had not raised his hopes.

"There's nothing you can do about it, Anne, thanks, anyway." He turned away again. "See you later," he said. Across the room, the old woman observed his approach with suspicion. She drew her heels up on the rung of her chair and clutched at her skirt, as if there was water on the floor.

Anne went to Harry Marvin for advice.

"You've been too protected," he said, answering her question. "You have no real knowledge of life, I mean. Why did you volunteer to work at Lime Rock? Why are you suddenly so concerned about Hamlin? Because you are interested medically in the patients? Or sociologically, even? Because you really want to help them? No. You came because your college education in the fine arts is worthless in any job which wouldn't bore you, and because you don't need a salary, and because a young girl ought to 'do something' while waiting to get married. People like you contribute nothing to society and therefore have an inner need for a cause. That's why you want to help him, Anne. You need a cause."

Satisfied with his diagnosis, he had walked away, as if nothing further need be said, as if her inquiry about Ernest Hamlin had not been of the slightest consequence. She wanted to run after him and boot him in the behind, having perceived that he resented the subject of Ernest Hamlin after her interruption of his speech this morning, and was sulking. Yet she was much less angry than hurt, for perhaps, in his cruelty, he had been right.

But was it so wrong, she thought, to want a cause? Or had he meant that her cause was selfish, false?

Unlike Mac and Sobel and the others, yes, and even

121

Harry Marvin, she could not quite accept the patients as sick human beings. Before her talks with Ernest Hamlin, they had been unreal to her, and her pity—which, until Harry intruded, she imagined had led her to volunteer—had remained intellectual. She had constantly to persuade herself that these people were not prisoners committed for the crime of lunacy. Weren't there bars on all the windows? And even the patients permitted out of doors were supervised and could not leave the grounds. In the afternoons they wandered about the hillside picking at things, like chickens. Or they sat immobile, hands clenched, on the benches, staring.

She could not regard them as the others did. The others astonished her. She had read somewhere, once long ago, that the staffs of mental hospitals were little more rational than the inmates, and were largely composed of sadists, perverts, misfits of all kinds. And in a way, this nonsensical idea struck her as more plausible than the selflessness she had come upon at Lime Rock Hospital. Yes, they were an ill-assorted lot, eccentric, even, some of them, but weren't the saints eccentric? It required a sort of saint, she thought, to work in a place like this for next to nothing, to rise above repulsion and sometimes fear, to love these mismade, badly broken creatures.

For in their separate ways, however tough or cynical or morbid, these people loved the patients. No other word described their attitude. Even the student nurses, younger than Anne and giggling, were finally seized by the same devotion, though chronic sufferers from nervous strain. As Mac had once remarked to Anne, "Even the veteran people here need a good, long weekend off now and again, but they come back."

I'd never come back, Anne had thought at the time. If I were weak enough to quit, I'd never find strength to return. But now, through Ernest Hamlin, she was nearing involvement in her work, and with it the dedication which sustained the others. She refused to be frightened off by Harry Marvin.

Anne sought out Dr. Sobel, who glanced over Hamlin's record. "What the patient has told you is true," Dr. Sobel started. "It's also true that he recognizes certain symptoms in advance, and reports them, so that these attacks can be to a certain extent controlled. But it isn't only a matter of recurrent pain, as he believes—"

"He's rational, then, Dr. Sobel, he's perfectly sane."

"Legally, perhaps. But apart from the pain he suffers—"

She didn't want to hear it. She said, "Then I think you should recommend that he be released in the custody of his doctor."

Dr. Sobel raised his eyebrows in alarm, clearly as surprised as she by her new candor. "I haven't the authority, Anne. And even if I had, I wouldn't use it."

"But you've just finished saying—"

"You won't let me finish," he said to her, smiling, and when she sat back in her chair, continued gently, "The fact remains that he has scraps of metal in the neural tissue. An operation is virtually out of the question. And that tissue may deteriorate."

"Well, until it does, I think he ought to be an outpatient. You say yourself that he reports the symptoms, and therefore isn't dangerous. You say—"

"He reports them today. But tomorrow? He's unpredictable, you see, and therefore must be regarded as mentally ill. He might get a crucial knock on the head, or his

123

personality might change entirely. The possibilities extend from idiocy to death. We just can't tell as yet."

"Does he know this?"

"Yes. I took his word for it that he wanted to know. He's a courageous man. But he can't believe it yet, poor fellow, and perhaps that's just as well."

Anne stared at him, still struggling with his previous remark. "I can't believe it myself," she whispered. "He's so normal, so healthy. He's healthier than I am."

Dr. Sobel parried her gaze with the shield of official jargon. "The hospital couldn't accept responsibility for his release," he said, and fingered his Phi Beta Kappa key.

Rising, she said, as if in afterthought, "And isn't it a more serious responsibility not to take a chance but to keep a patient here unfairly?"

"Half the patients here are here unfairly, Anne. You yourself must know a dozen people now at large who might replace those in your ward. Some of our eccentric old people, some of the children, some of the retarded— there'd be places for all of them in secure or unselfish homes. There's no place for Hamlin in any home."

She ran into Harry Marvin outside. It was almost as if he had determined to follow her around, to badger her. He apologized for his rudeness, however, and displayed concern about what Dr. Sobel had had to say.

"That's right," he said, when she had finished. "This is a state hospital, and state appointees must place their responsibilities to the public, the voting public, that is, above the fate of this individual, this unimportant individual. Mental hospitals are a bum investment, they don't pay off politically, as Mac says."

"What do you mean, unimportant individual? Didn't he

fight for his country? Isn't that why he's here? How can you say—"

"You're very young, Anne, and very naïve. Nobody in Lime Rock is important, politically or otherwise, or they wouldn't be here. This man Hamlin of yours is an ex-machinist. If he was an ex-alderman, the son of an ex-alderman, or knew the son of an ex-alderman, or even an ex-policeman, he'd be at home, at least until he hurt somebody."

"I don't believe it!"

"I can't help it if you don't. But it's the truth. There's a kid in the Monkey House who's only here because he was *born* here, how do you like that? To a schizo prostitute who died. Who's going to speak up for him? I looked into it, and I got the story that the foundling homes are already overcrowded, and that he might as well be left here until he's old enough to go to school. By that time he will probably be very well qualified to stay right where he is."

"You just looked into it, is that it? You didn't try to do anything about it."

"As a matter of fact, I did. But not too hard. I didn't risk losing my job over it, and that's because there are too few of us willing to work here. Trained people, that is," he added, pointedly. "In other words, I'm no use to these people if I'm outside."

"I wish I had your self-confidence," Anne snapped, outraged.

"Oh, you'll have it," Harry said, "when you've been here a little while." He glided effortlessly over her sarcasm. "And I'm glad to see you taking such an interest in a patient, by the way. Do you really care what happens to him?"

125

"Yes, I do. I admire him. I told him I'd try to help him, and I will."

"You *told* him that?"

"Yes, I did."

"You've made a bad mistake."

"I know I have," Anne said. She fled before the tears came.

"Never mind Harry," Mac told her later. "He's fine with those children, and he works very hard, but he's a little nervous about his importance here. That's why he takes it out on you, I think. He's possessive about the place, for some reason. In fact, just between you and me, he's god-damned neurotic and no mistake." She jammed her cigarette into her coffee cup. "We all are, I guess. The longer you work here the more clearly you recognize the very fine line between ourselves and the patients. Sometimes there's no line at all, or rather, people cross it, back and forth, back and forth, from both sides. When you see that, and see that mental illness is largely a matter of degree, then you can identify yourself with the patients, and work with all your heart."

Anne nodded. "I think I know what you mean, now, after talking to Ernest Hamlin."

"Perhaps you do," Mac said shortly. Her statement of faith of a moment before had made her uncomfortable. "The other thing that I wanted to say to you was that Harry was right—you *have* made a mistake. But we've all made that mistake here when our emotions got involved. It only happens to you once. It takes just once to learn. So just forget it."

Anne nodded again. "And you can't help him either, Mac?"

"I'll give it a try," Mac said.

She went to see the director. "I tried," she reported to Anne the following day. "Old Silvertongue said he understood the unhappy predicament of the patient, but that his own hands were tied. He said this Hamlin was committed through the Veterans Hospital, that it might be called a federal affair. He also said that, while of course he was grateful for my services, I might reflect on the fact that I have no medical training and am hardly in a position to contest the decision of qualified doctors. He set me straight, in short." Mac shrugged her shoulders. "Give it up, kid. Life's too short to get angry about injustice, in this place or out of it. Sobel's Augean Stable is the world. I've been angry since I came here, fifteen years ago, and all I've got to show for it is ulcers."

ERNEST HAMLIN CAME every day to the occupational therapy unit and worked unceasingly with the other patients. If, at first, they resented what they considered to be presumption on the part of their fellow sufferer, they soon came to depend on him, and were cross and quarrelsome during two days when he did not appear. Anne did not ask him where he had been, nor did she have to, since his haggard face told her all she needed to know. And he only said, smiling, "That was kind of a bad one," en route to a discussion of grandchildren with a hazy old woman who did not realize that these very grandchildren of whom she was so proud had seen to it that she would end her days at Lime Rock State Mental Hospital.

Unlike Anne, Ernest could make these people laugh. She could not quite understand how he went about it, except that he made of himself a sort of gift, a plaything. He was their friend and confessor, but he was also their scapegoat, shuffleboard victim, and willing butt of their strange humor. The room rang with cries of "Ernie, Ernie!," as if only he, like a big blond Peter Pan, could bring to life their makeshift games.

Anne, too, now enjoyed her work; she, too, depended on him. She took such pleasure in his company that at times she forgot or put aside the remembrance that he was waiting for her help. For though he never once mentioned her offer or alluded to it, she sensed that his happy efforts with the patients were in part inspired by the possibility of his own deliverance, a possibility held out by Anne and Anne alone, and that he had to struggle to keep from questioning her about her progress.

And of course she had made no progress, had, in fact, given up. Once, in exasperation at her helplessness, she had tried to parcel out the burden of her blame. "What about your mother?" she had said to Ernie. "Does she come to visit you?"

He had been uncomfortable. "No," he said, and after a moment, "The trip is kind of hard for her. She's kind of old and she ain't got too much money, see." He stopped. "I don't know, to tell you the honest-to-God truth. I thought maybe she might make it up here once or twice, but she didn't."

"But your fiancée—wouldn't she come if you wrote to her? Or at least encourage your mother to come if she couldn't come herself?"

"No, not her. She'd do just the opposite, I guess. If Ma comes, she's got to come, too, or else feel bad about not coming. She ain't mean or nothing, only a little selfish, just between you and me."

128

"But I thought you were in love with her."

"No, I never said that. I kind of *had* to marry her, for old time's sake, because of the way we were before I went to Korea." He blushed and, blushing, added, "After knowing you, I couldn't marry her no more anyway."

She had guessed already that he thought himself in love with her, and she in turn admired him, depended on him, yes, and "loved" him, if that were the same thing. So now they faced each other, breathless.

"Thanks," said her voice, too loudly, jauntily. "You're not so bad yourself." She had inherited her mother's habit of turning beet red in the face. Later she told herself that she had flirted with him selfishly, thus compounding her earlier crime.

"Ernie," she said another day, determined to have it out with him, "there's nothing I can do to help you. I've talked to people, and the director knows about it, even, and they all say the same thing—it has to be worked through the Veterans Hospital."

She could not bear to look at his face until he spoke. "Anne, I told you that before, I told you there ain't nothing you can do." His voice was unnaturally calm. She peered at him. He was trying to smile, but some vital element was dying in his face, shifting and fading like the bright colors of a fish. He stood transfixed before her, unaware of a shrill voice from across the room.

"Ernie, Ernie! Shuffleboard! Ernie, Ernie!"

She started to cry, and he came forward and took her hand.

"Why am I crying?" she mumbled, enraged at herself. "I'm being so silly, Ernie. You just have to write that hospital and ask for a review of your case, that's all . . ."

"That's all," Ernie said.

". . . and it won't be long before they develop some safe new operating technique, you'll be out of here in no time." She wiped her eyes and attempted a cheerful smile.

"That's right," Ernie said.

She had never seen such an expression in her life.

She plunged onward, hopelessly. "And you've got to be careful in the meantime, Ernie, not to bump your head, you've got to have patience and courage."

"How did you know about my head?" Ernie said.

"Dr. Sobel. You've got to be very careful, you've got to—"

"Dr. Sobel. He's okay, Doc Sobel." Ernie nodded his head. "Thanks anyway. I'll see you later."

"Where are you going?"

"Don't you hear them calling to me? I'm going to play shuffleboard with the boys."

"Ernie!"

He waited.

"Ernie, everything's going to work out fine! And afterwards, maybe you and I, we can celebrate together—"

She saw that instant that she had made still another mistake. Instead of cheering him, she had made him face the facts, Dr. Sobel's facts, and his face quivered on the point of tears. He turned and fled, and she did not talk to him again.

Anne found a student nurse to take her place. She went for a walk between the rufous buildings, driven faster and faster until she found herself running, going nowhere. The day was cold, it was nearly December now, and the sharp air seared her lungs.

130   Afterwards, Ernie came less frequently to her ward.

When he did come, he avoided her, and she did not seek him out. She had only worsened things with every effort to assist him, and was frightened of her own ineptitude. Yet she watched him, and when he imagined she was not looking he watched her. He helped with the patients less and less, and they in turn called out to him less, as if they now included him in their ranks and meant to treat him with the same suspicion and superiority with which, unpersuaded of their own conditions, they treated the other sick around them. Only once she went to him and asked him how he felt, and he said shortly, "I feel dandy." In the way that, once, his presence in the ward had given her confidence, it now inhibited her.

She was startled by her new assertive self, the self that stood up to Harry Marvin, tried to bully Dr. Sobel, coerced poor Mac into visiting the director. True, it had brought her confidence when she needed it most, and she had Ernest Hamlin to thank for this. But it had also betrayed her into errors she would never before have had the courage to consider.

Harry Marvin was right, she told herself. I don't belong here.

ONE NIGHT EARLY IN DECEMBER she was awakened by the telephone and made her way downstairs to answer it. "We need everyone out here, Anne," came Harry's voice, trying not to sound excited. "We've got an emergency on our hands."

"I'll be right there," Anne said aloud, although he had hung up already.

It was nearly midnight.

On the highway by the main gate were a number of cars

with motors running. A state policeman held up a white-gloved hand in the beam of her headlights.

"Authorized personnel only, miss."

"I'm a volunteer worker here. They telephoned me."

Their voices were loud in a noise like heavy wind. He consulted a list.

"No Pryor listed, miss. Authorized personnel only. You better move your car, miss, you're blocking the entrance."

"Officer, they need people up there, they telephoned me—"

"C'mon, girlie, I told you once, no sightseers, no visitors. I got my orders! Now let's move along!"

"I'm not a sightseer! I work here, I really do!" Anne's voice broke, she was shaking with nervousness and cold as a second angry officer came forward and Mac drew up alongside.

"McKittredge, Miss Adelaide," Mac barked, seeing the list. "What's the matter, Anne?"

The second officer said, "Oh, Jesus," and waved Anne after Mac. She drove haltingly through the milling faces, which were shouting above the din, a din which rose out of the night behind the trees. Then she traced Mac's blood-red taillights, which cut up the hill into the darkness like two fast angry insects. Her heart moved violently, and she felt sick.

There were lights in the Administration Building but the other shapes crouched back into the night. People ran in all directions. "They've cut the lights," Mac shouted in Anne's ear. She had a cigarette stub in her mouth, trotting clumsily along the driveway.

"What's happening, what's happening!" Anne cried, her voice picked up and whirled away in the avalanche of noise, a noise of endless feet in flight across a waste of concrete, of objects smashed against high iron windows, a noise of screaming.

The sound ricocheted around among the buildings, breaking out to surge like wind along the barren hillside, down across the frozen winter woods, the highway, and the town beyond.

Anne was sent with a student nurse to help in the children's ward. They ran together over the bare ground, forsaking the cement sidewalks.

"What's happening!" Anne cried again. "What's happening!"

"Rioting!" the girl shrieked back at her. "It started in the men's wards and spread all over!" The girl was beside herself with excitement, yet apparently unafraid. "We've got the doors locked, they can't get out, but they're breaking everything, the director says, he's getting the fire trucks up here with fire hoses!"

The children's wards were nearly under control. The children had been herded into corners. Most of them were badly frightened, and some of these were hysterical and screaming. A few were still running wild, hurling clothes and toothbrushes and bedpans; one little boy kicked furiously at an idiot huddled by the broken window. A big nurse reached him and he cursed and struck at her. Like most of the others he was naked in the winter drafts which swept the room. This little boy was named Robert Esposito, and he still bore scars inflicted by his father before and after he had finally set fire to his school.

Anne went from there to the women's wards. Here, too, the worst of the riot was over, and she wondered fleetingly if she would ever find a chance to be of use. The clothes

133

of the women had been ripped to pieces, and they wandered aimless in their nudity, complaining. One was in a catatonic state and had attached herself, in frenzy, to another. The victim was a nice old woman known as Happy who was sent lollipops from home. She suffered a slight heart attack as the other woman was pried from her. Helping the frail body to a bed, Anne smelled the forsaken age of her and knew at last the love for these patients that the others felt. "Ah, dearie, thank you," the old woman gasped. "It isn't fit for folks like us to see such terrible sights, and I thank the Good Lord that my children never will."

By five in the morning, the men's wards had been subjugated. The midnight dark was turning towards a winter gray. Anne, standing in the cold, smoked a solitary cigarette and wondered about Ernest Hamlin. Before her the fire trucks, red lights still flashing, backed across the frozen earth, and the hoses nosed through the end doors of the buildings. The men inside were shouting still and pounding the bars on the upper floors, but the cries were more protesting now and less excited. The roar sagged slowly to a fretful moan and finally to a whine, until only now and then a metal object clanked without spirit on the bars, and the water pumps on the fire trucks commandeered the silence of December dawn. She learned from Harry later that an old man named Herbie Collins had been hurled against the wall by the rush of water and had died within minutes of a fractured skull.

"Poor old Collins staggered into the way," Harry Marvin said, "but that hose was aimed at your friend Ernest Hamlin." Harry was drawn and in need of a shave, and upset about Robert Esposito, who had been making progress, Harry said, considering the fact that twice before being sent to Lime Rock he had been hospitalized after discipline by his father.

They were having coffee in the basement of the Administration Building.

"Why Ernest?" Anne said.

"Because he started the whole business. The guy with the hose didn't know that, of course, he only saw that this big ox with the plumbing pipe in his hand and pounding his head against the wall was the man to stop. That's why."

"How is he?"

"Who?"

"Ernie."

"I don't know how Ernie is. I don't care how Ernie is. I care about Robert Esposito and poor old Collins."

"He's hurt himself," Dr. Sobel told her, and his interruption was a clear rebuke to Harry. He had been silent until now, staring at his coffee. "Hamlin had an attack, and he didn't give us warning. I think he knew he was going to have it. I think he hit his head on purpose. But," he said to Harry Marvin, "I don't think he started the riot on purpose. What he did to himself frightened the others, got them excited."

"That's right," another doctor said. "I talked to one of my patients in there. He said this Hamlin started yelling, that he got into the washroom and wrenched this pipe loose and started breaking things. Then the men in his ward got excited and started yelling for help, and the other wards just sort of picked it up. Of course certain patients joined Hamlin in pounding on the bars and breaking, it was a release for them in a way, and finally the whole place was infected. Like a plague."

"Where is he now?" Anne whispered.

135

"We have him under phenobarb," a nurse said briskly. "He's upstairs right now, in the in-patients room. But we're transferring him to the disturbed ward."

"He's going to stay there, too," Harry Marvin said.

"He's hurt himself. I don't know why, but he's hurt himself. On purpose." Dr. Sobel tapped a small sad finger on his temple. "Probably permanently. I've talked to him already."

"Did he hurt anybody else?"

"No," Harry Marvin snapped. "Just got them killed, is all. He was much too normal, as you know, to hurt anybody."

"Harry," Mac said, "why don't you shut up?" She got to her feet and left the room, and Anne followed her.

"I'd like to see him, Mac," she said.

Mac nodded approvingly.

"Good for you, go right ahead. He's receiving, as you know, in the in-patients room. Poor bastard." She banged through the supply room door.

Anne climbed the stairs and went to see Ernest Hamlin. His head was on a pillow, bandaged, and his body was strapped to the metal cot. When she entered the room, he opened his eyes and constructed a sort of smile.

"I made it, kid," he said. "The varsity shuffleboard team." He started to laugh, a laughter high like crying. Then he frowned. "They hurt me in there. I told you they were out to get me because I wasn't nuts like them, and now they hurt me. My head hurts, see. They knew it was dangerous for me to hurt my head, and they hurt me anyway!"

He seemed surprised.

"Who, Ernie?" She wanted to reach out to him but could not. Through the window behind him she could see the fringe of trees down to the east, etched black by the sharp rising light of winter sun, and she thought, Beyond there, far away, the outside world encircles us and pins us in.

"They. Those guys. All those guys."

"The doctors, you mean? The firemen?"

"Yeah, everybody," Ernest Hamlin muttered. "Them, too. All those guys." He was staring straight at the white ceiling, frowning, and took no notice of her when she bent and pressed her forehead to the cool iron of his cot.

1963

ON THE RIVER STYX

On the pale flats the lone trace of man was a leaning stake marking some lost channel that a storm or shift of current had filled in. On the end of the stake perched a ragged cormorant, its drying wings held wide in a black cross against the wind. The archaic bird, the rampant mangroves, the hidden underwater life raising ghostly puffs from the white marl dust of ages of dead creatures, deepened Burkett's sense of solitude, of pointlessness. Earlier that day they had seen a silver horizon off to the west, where the Ten Thousand Islands opened out onto the Gulf, and this window of light, for a little while, had dissipated a vague dread that had been gathering for days.

The marl reaches were too shallow for the outboard, and the skiff moved so quietly across the flats that Burkett could hear the minute fret of water on the hull.

Facing astern, he tried to befriend the black man standing on the thwart, who always worked as if he were sneaking up on something, even in the open water, staring about him, catching his breath, as if emptiness itself were a thing to fear. On his sculling pole, leaning out over the stern, as far away from the white people as possible, the bony figure— the shadowed face under the straw hat, the tattered shoulder of his faded shirt, the unnameable odor—swung in arcs on the hot white sky, back and forth and forth and back against the wild green walls. The water, browned by mangrove tannin, turned gray when the sun clouded over, and the dark islets spread away, parted, regathered, always surrounding. With their silent boatman, his wife had said, it was like traveling the River Styx.

Behind him, Alice sat unprotesting in the bow. Her rag-doll smile, still pretty and fresh at forty-three, required no lipstick, and she rarely wore it. Why, he wondered, had she worn it to go fishing? The red smear of lipstick on her bucktooth, the funny sun hat, the white sun paste on her nose, the incongruous earphones of the tape player clutched too tightly in her hand—her eccentric aspect intensified his instinct that they had no place here. (She knew what she looked like and performed a whimsical fishing routine when he asked how she was doing, brandishing her rod, crying fiercely, "Fisher Woman!") If only for her sake— since she was no fisherman—they should have gone deep-sea fishing out of Fort Lauderdale, or bonefishing out of Islamorada in the Keys, where there were friendly people to relax with, drink with, where she might have spent a day around the pool. In this wild region the inhabitants held them away, even this guide, who was too makeshift in his

139

preparations to bring along his lunch and too uneasy to accept a part of theirs.

Burkett, who had his own small boat at home near the Potomac, was rather proud of his knowledge of boats and fishing. It seemed absurd to pay good money to sit in this hard skiff and be poled around in these godforsaken mangroves hauling in ladyfish and snappers when what he had come for was the robalo, or "snook." "He has his heart set on a *snook*," Alice had informed their friends in Washington, where he was a lawyer for the Interior Department. When Alice said that she understood why tourists might go elsewhere, he retorted crossly that they were fishermen, not tourists. To this, in the face of the gloomy discomfort of the guide, she hollered, "Fisher Woman! Snook!" (pronouncing it *snewk* in the local accent, yanking her rod back to set the hook, and battling the fierce snook to a standstill with eyes closed in a reckless parody of her own sexual abandon, to get him to laugh at himself, which at last he did).

At least the town was an inexpensive place that they could talk about entertainingly when they got home. An old-time Indian trading post from the days of commerce in otter pelts and egret plumes, this small fishing settlement at the far end of an eight-mile canal road was the "last frontier town" at the edge of "the last wilderness" of the Ten Thousand Islands. Here was a stronghold of the vanishing snook, and here hard-bitten shrimp and mullet fishermen—according to well-informed colleagues over at the Justice Department—grew rich on night runs of marijuana through this shallow-water archipelago, where patrol boats came to grief when they tried to follow, where new pickup trucks and limousines left for Miami from weathered cottages on the cracked and grassy streets of an old Gulf Coast town that lacked a decent restaurant, much less a movie house. The Burketts had seen no sign of limousines, but it was certainly true about the movie house. As for the fried food in the motel café, Alice said, it had been freshly reheated every day since the Civil War. In the evenings, owing to mosquito plagues, they could not walk the quiet streets under the palms. Instead they confronted a black-and-white TV in a dim, bare room that stank of disinfect-ant. Days and nights alike were hot and humid, and the nearest beach, a patch of sand among the mangrove roots, three miles away by boat down the main channel, was beaten hard by the gray and windy water of the Gulf.

At each new evidence that they had erred, Alice would gaze at him in wonder. Why didn't her loving husband get her out of here? He didn't stay merely out of stubbornness; he had some idea about getting to know these people. But these people had no wish to be known. That he kept trying, she supposed, had something to do with self-respect, with persevering to avoid some obscure defeat. Anyway, she did not expect him to explain to her what he scarcely under-stood himself. His first snook would justify the trip, and he had to admit he was sort of curious about the rumored drug trade, which might account for the suspicion with which they had been received.

Alice said that he was paranoid, these lovable folks were just standoffish with strangers. Like most Americans—she informed him—he couldn't tolerate feeling unwelcome: "You cracker bastards gonna love us whether ya like us or not!" Alice declared, shaking her fist at the silent commu-nity outside their cabin.

For all her clowning, Alice shared his own uneasiness.   141

She sat there hunched up on her seat, having an eager, frightened time. With the dour black man looming over them—like a hanged man in the wind, said Alice—she rarely spoke, except for occasional mild exclamations about the confetti of white egrets on the green walls, or the sentinel herons that stood far out on the shallow water, waiting for—what? The coasting rays, small barracuda, the pale crabs turning up their claws as the boat passed—everything out on the white flats seemed to watch and wait.

She had a horror of the bottom life, the myriad amorphous things acting out silent destinies and violent ends in shrouds of underwater dust, and could scarcely bring herself to look over the side. At home she loved her bird feeders and garden. So much impenetrable growth, so many gaunt huge bleak-eyed birds, oppressed her. The sonatas of Europe on her tape recorder protected her from the great New World silence.

As for the boatman, he was inclined to silence even when spoken to. Most fishing guides were easygoing guys, and the best of them made the client feel like a real fishing partner. But Dickie's discolored eyes were evasive, unamused; most of the time he whistled tunelessly under his breath. ("When he's *really* uneasy," Alice said, "he sounds like a tea kettle.") They assumed that this had something to do with being a black man in a backwater town bypassed in the fight for civil rights. The black people lived in their own community several miles up the canal road toward the state highway, and were unwelcome in Seminole after dark, as Burkett discovered on the evening of their arrival when he tried to locate a fishing guide for the next day. He made no attempt to conceal his surprise, which was instantly perceived as disapproval. "Jest seem to be the way them folks prefers it," he was warned by "Judge" Jim Whidden, the owner of the Calusa Motel and unelected leader of the town. "Ain't no *law* about it, mister. Maybe they ain't exactly *in*tegrated, but they ain't discriminated, neither, not the way you people think."

Asked the next day about the black community, the guide glowered and grinned at the same time and did not answer, pretending that the white man had made a joke. Annoyed by his wife's warning poke, Burkett persisted. His feeling was that, as a representative of the U.S. government, he should probably report the matter to his colleagues over at Justice. But it turned out that the guide was proud of his own status as Whidden's servant. In fact, he slept in the "Whidden Buildin" on nights when he helped out in the café. "All de res' of 'em haves to go home. Guess dass de way dat cullud folks prefers it, jes' like Judge Jim say." Burkett had hoped that Dickie would relax once he understood that their concern about the situation was sincere, that they had marched in the civil rights demonstrations in the sixties, and that any confidence he might make to them was safe. Instead, their friendliness intensified his fear of them. He seemed more skittish every day.

Because none of the mangrove islets had dry land, they went ashore at midday on one of the spoil banks of white marl and fossil shell along the channel to the open Gulf used by the fishing boats and a few private craft. Here Alice could stretch her legs a little, and go behind a bush. But the dry marl was baked hard, there was no place for her to sunbathe, and with Dickie nearby, sighing with hunger, they felt obliged to share both food and conversation.

One day Burkett brought along their bottle of rum, to make the trip slightly more festive. Because it was awkward to exclude the guide, he ignored his wife's raised eyebrows and offered Dickie a drink, well mixed with tonic. Dickie looked startled, but he did not turn it down. He even smiled after a pleasant interlude, asking Alice if he might listen through her earphones. Clearly she had mixed feelings about this, but she handed them over cheerfully enough, and Dickie enjoyed a little Mozart. He asked how much the tape player cost, and when she said uncomfortably, "Oh, a couple hundred dollars," he gave in to an impending fit of nervous laughter. "You bes' tip me *good,* ah gone get *me* one!" Exhilarated by the first social occasion they had enjoyed since they had arrived, Burkett included Dickie in a second round, which Alice refused to share.

Dickie put down his empty glass, sighed, shook his head, and smiled. "You folks wants somethin in dis ol' town, you jes' ask Dickie," he said, excited. "I de number-one cullud around here, de number-one." Still smiling, he glanced from one to the other. Then—neither forthright nor furtive—his long hand slipped slowly as a snake into the basket and removed a sandwich. Having gone this far, he lost his nerve, and dared not eat in front of them. He cocked his head toward the rumble of a boat motor behind the islands, and on this pretext, swaying and laughing, moved away to do something with the skiff.

Burkett was always aroused by rum and the smell of sunburn cream; he wanted to touch his wife. But Alice was intent on Dickie. Against the water shine that haloed his dark head, they could see the silhouette of earphones, as if he were tuned in to outer space.

She shifted, restless, under his hand. "Listen, I love your idealism, and your curiosity and good intentions. I do. How else could I have married a damn bureaucrat?" She took his hand to soften what was coming. "But I think what you're doing with Dickie is stupid as hell." She waved away his protest. "You just don't have to come on so hard as his white fishing buddy. I think you should stick to catching that weird snewk."

The wall of islands parted to release a broad white boat. High in the bow, with a deckhouse and a long low work deck, she threw a deep wake that struck the spoil banks of white shell on either side of the narrow channel. The wave carried outward, slapping noisily into the mangroves.

Burkett watched the boat through binoculars. He grinned when he saw someone with binoculars observing him through the deckhouse window. The unused nets had a new linen color, and unlike other shrimp boats they had seen, this one seemed to ride too high out of the water. Burkett waved to a pale man in a black T-shirt who came out on deck. The man did not wave back, and Burkett jumped to grab the rum bottle and basket as the boat's wake surged high onto the spoil bank, washing down again with a brittle tinkling of old shells.

"Sonofabitch! No shrimps in *that* boat!" he cried out to the guide.

Refloating the skiff, Dickie stared off in the wrong direction.

"You see that?" Burkett demanded of his wife, who raised her eyebrows, gazing after the departing boat as if she had missed something. "See how clean she looks? That shrimper never carried *shrimps,* I'll tell you that!"

"You don't know that. You just want to believe it because you're my square darling and you're a little drunk and it would make your vacation more exciting for some reason."

145

"Goddamnit, Alice, they run enough dope through this place to turn on the whole state—" He checked his outburst, seeing Dickie standing there holding the skiff. Angry, he said, "Goddamnit, Dickie, tell her what that boat is *really* used for!"

The black man was silent for a moment.

"Shrimp boat, suh."

"How come she rides so high out of the water? Pretty light cargo, wouldn't you say? And how come she's heading out so late in the day?"

"New boat, suh. Jes' checkin her out, what dey calls shakedown." Dickie steadied the skiff as they got in. "Shrimps comes to de surface in de night. Fish dem at night."

Burkett winked at his drinking companion, but Dickie's face had closed again, and his wife's face was closed, too. He resented her superior attitude, but he also knew he had behaved stupidly, and he got into the skiff in a foul humor. In the afternoon sun, the rum had given him a headache. He prodded a mangrove snapper with a sneakered toe. The gray fish lay stiff on the skiff floorboards, mouth stretched painfully.

The tide was low when they got back, and the dogs, old people, and children, moving out of the shadows of a giant banyan, stared straight down at the sun-parched foreigners with the red knees and comic hats. Every day this small convocation included old dock fishermen in tractor caps wearing bright white T-shirts under nylon shirts despite hot weather, and a washed-out child with one hand on a smaller brother and the other jammed between her legs.

Rum-and-sun-struck, Burkett rose, spreading his hands for balance. The folks laughed. "Give you a hand, Dickie?" he said.

"Nosuh." Dickie braced the skiff and waited, averting his gaze from them as if ashamed. He seemed to efface himself against the bulkhead. The onlookers murmured when Burkett, helping his wife onto the dock, had to push her buttocks from below, exposing the painful red line between thigh and hip ("Beach or no beach," she had said, "I'm not going home without a tan!") and again when she clambered a little way on hands and knees before rising and turning, waiting for Dickie to hand up their gear. "Ahs got 'em," Dickie said ungraciously. He had not offered to take their things the day before, and later they attributed his new-found manners to the presence of Judge Jim Whidden. Arms folded on his rolling chest, Judge Jim observed them from an overturned boat under the banyan.

Whidden rose and tipped a pearl-gray hat. He was a fat man but not soft, with a strong face hard-packed in lard, and a twitch of humor.

"You folks make out all right?"

"No snook yet," Burkett said. "Nice snappers, though."

"Why, that's fine, Lawyer, that's fine. We'll fry 'em up for you this evenin." Judge Jim beamed from one to the other. "Dickie take care of you good?" The man's big voice carried easily to Dickie and the onlookers, and Burkett started down the dock, unable to focus or dispel his irritation and anxious to remove himself from the whole scene.

"Oh, Dickie was fine!" Alice was saying, with the haunted look she always wore when she had to pee.

Judge Jim caught Burkett's elbow as he went past. "I told him take care of you folks good when you first come here. Ain't a nigger in town knows them holes like Dickie there." He gave Burkett a confiding wink. "Or Nigra, neither." To the onlookers, he said heartily, "Got to take care of our tourists good, y'know, bein as how we ain't got hardly

147

any!" He patted Burkett's shoulder, setting him free, in sign that this afternoon's jokes and hospitality were at an end.

Whidden's tossed chins commanded Dickie to get these people's stuff up to their cabin. Burkett thanked Dickie, who hurried past them. Aware of being watched, they walked up the street to the cabin on the white sand yard behind the "Whidden Building," two stories of worn white clapboard that housed post office, the Judge's office, and the kitchen, bar, and restaurant of the Calusa Motel.

At the door of their cottage they were welcomed by the yard man, who presented them with the baskets left by Dickie. As far as the Burketts could determine, this small black Johnny in red sneakers had the only friendly face in town. "We gone fix dem snappuhs *nice* fo' you! Dass right! In de ol'-time way."

Alice squirmed past and rushed into the bathroom, which had a hook lock, a pink plastic tub, and a wide gap under the door. When she emerged, poking her hair, the funny hat and the white paste were gone. "You're getting a nice tan," he said, to cheer her. Acting pleased, she raised her fingertips to her fiery brow, and touched by her gallantry, he said by way of apology, "I guess I thought there would be other people here, someone to talk to."

She nodded brightly, and he went into the bathroom, still fuzzy from the rum at noon. How sick he was of drinking rum from thin bathroom glasses, in the long evenings confined to this damn cabin! They couldn't even sit outside because of all the holes in their porch screen, and nowhere else in town did they feel welcome.

Poor old Fisher Woman, he thought, with a rush of affection. We'll make love.

She was sitting on the bed edge, the lunch basket in her

lap, as if trying to remember something. She ignored his fingertips on her neck. "Dickie forgot to bring the rum," she said. "It's not in the basket." Her voice had an edge, but she shrugged off his inquiry.

"Hell, I'll go get it," he said, bothered, too.

"Be careful," she murmured unaccountably, following him out onto the porch, and he made a pantomime of fighting off giant mosquitoes, which did not amuse her. "I mean, don't get him in trouble," she called after him. He stopped.

"Why not?" he said. He told her his new opinion of the guide, how much he disliked this sullen ungrateful man. Wasn't it patronizing and hypocritical, wasn't it reverse racism, to indulge a shifty-eyed sonofabitch like that just because he was black?

He expected her to defend Dickie but she said quietly, "I don't like him either. He's sneaky and he's aggressive. I've watched how he sucks up to Whidden and how he bullies that nice Johnny, and the old lady who cleans up. The man's a fascist, or at least a shit." When her husband laughed, she said, "But maybe we encouraged him or something, okay? So don't get him in trouble."

He went down to check the boat, certain now that the search would be in vain. When he climbed back up onto the dock, a thin local man in a worn felt hat and white long-sleeved Sunday shirt buttoned at the neck was standing there under the banyan, hands in hip pockets. His flat gaze warned the stranger that he had his eye on him. Burkett almost explained what he was doing in the boat. Instead he said sharply, "Can I help you?"

The man bared his upper teeth, to suck them. He watched Burkett go.

Up the street, laughing and frowning simultaneously, Johnny agreed that it was a nice evening. He said he was waiting for his ride, that he did not know where Dickie was. His gaze darted up and down the street.

It was near twilight, the mosquitoes were convening, and by the time Burkett reached the bar door of the café, he was running. He jumped through the screen door and yanked it shut.

Without taking their eyes off Burkett, two men on the point of leaving moved back among the tables in the rear, feeling behind them for their chairs. They sank down slowly, watched him with the others, not with hostility or curiosity, but in the same relentless way they had watched the plastic colors of the TV screen over the bar.

The front end of the bar was strewn with a litter of candy and cigarettes and peanuts, and the shot bottles were lined up on a shelf behind. A dark outline marked the former location of a mirror. On three unattached stools at the far end perched three old men in stained straw hats. They were drinking beer with an old woman who sat on a fourth stool behind the bar. Because the stranger appeared to be looking for somebody, she did not come forward, and Dickie, who was wiping off an empty table, refused to let Burkett catch his eye. Their eyes met for a single moment as, gathering up abandoned glasses, he drank one off defiantly between bar and kitchen. Then the door swung to behind him.

Cocking his head to observe the stranger, one of the old men pushed his hat back. "Lemme have one of them beers," he muttered. The old woman reached back into the cooler without turning around and fished him out a bottle, which he opened carefully with a knife. "I reckon this here is number eight." The old man looked at the bottle with surprise, turning it slowly in his hand.

The woman nodded. "Close onto it, anyways," she grunted.

Dickie did not reappear, and Burkett shifted from one foot to the other, intent on the old advertising cards for plug tobaccos.

"I guess you know it ain't me is gonna pay for it." The old man worked the wet label from the bottle with his thumb, looking belligerent.

"Judge Jim don't give a good goddamn who pays. You talk to Jim."

"Why, goddamnit to hell, my *boy* takes care of me! Makes more than he know how to spend! He told me, 'Pap, go drink it up, and welcome!'"

She glanced at Burkett. "He'd tell you, 'Pap, you shut up your fool mouth,' if he was here." She climbed off her stool and shuffled down the bar to Burkett, who realized that Dickie was not going to come back.

"Yessir. Coffee? Black or integrated?"

"Up north, them people like their coffee *in*tegrated," one of the old men insisted when Burkett ignored the woman's bait. "That's what Judge Jim says."

"I'd like a bottle of rum, if that's all right."

"All right by me, but we ain't got none. Ain't got but Seven Crown and John Begg, leastways in fifths."

"Seven Crown is fine."

The old woman raised her voice as a service to the customers. "What brand you folks use up there in Washington, D.C.?"

To encourage his conversation, she sat down on the bar and folded her arms across an old blue dress. In the silence, he could hear the hum of flies against the ceiling.

"I guess Mr. Whidden told you where we were from."

151

"Judge tole me hisself yest'day morning. That's my boy, you know. Run this café for him."

"Well, well," Burkett said. "So he's a judge."

"Yep. Judge enough fer us." She looked at him closely. "We ain't got no federal men round here. Don't have much call fer 'em."

He laughed. "I'm just a lawyer up there. Environmental lawyer."

"Ain't got much law around here, neither." This time she cackled, and the chairs shifted. "Judge Jim pretty well takes care of what law they is."

"I guess I'll take that Seven Crown then, Mrs. Whidden."

"Your money, mister."

When she returned from the back room, the people watched Burkett take his change and the bottle of whiskey. "Don't need no Seven-Up with your Seven Crown? We get a lot of call for Seven and Seven."

He shook his head. "Goodnight," he said.

"Come see us, hear?" She spoke over her shoulder.

"WELCOME TO GLORIOUS Snook City!" To keep his spirits up, he gestured grandly through the skimpy curtains at the huge red sun in the black archipelago to westward and the long string of evening ibis, flapping and sailing down the sky. Opening the whiskey, he described his adventures to Alice, who was still distracted and did not laugh as he had hoped.

"You'd think," she said, "they'd have a nice saloon, to attract snewk-ers."

"They don't *want* to attract snewk-ers, and guess why? Did you see Dickie's face today when I pointed out that

152

ON THE RIVER STYX

so-called shrimp boat?" Burkett poured himself a darker
drink than usual and drank it with a loud gasp of relief.

"Maybe that *was* just a shrimp boat. Maybe you should
forget this whole drug business. What would they do to
Dickie if they thought he told you?"

"Hell, they're not hiding it. I told you about that old guy
in the bar." Feeling irritable again, he rattled the ice in his
thin glass. "Anyway, I thought you didn't like him."

"I don't," she said, frowning at her drink. "But I've
decided it's societal conditioning. He's been warped by
heartless capitalist oppression."

He refilled his drink and gazed out at the sunset, sighing.

"Stop stalling," she said quietly, after a pause. "Did that
Negro gentleman swipe our hootch, or didn't he?"

"We have to give him the benefit of the doubt."

"Okay. Because my tape recorder's missing, too."

"You must have left it in the boat."

"You *looked* in the boat, remember?"

"He couldn't be that crazy, Alice! In *this* town?"

"Maybe he didn't steal it. He didn't steal that sandwich,
either. Maybe he just took it."

"I'm just not going to accuse him, that's all!"

"That's the point right there. That's what he knows."

"He couldn't count on that. He wouldn't chance it."

"A man might chance anything if he was angry enough.
And drunk."

"You *really* believe that?"

"I believe he took my tape deck, isn't that enough? And
you do, too."

Burkett was silent. He thought about those people in the
bar, and Dickie's reckless rage, gulping that drink. He
thought about the man in the white Sunday shirt, down by   153

the boat. He thought of the big man in his pearl-gray fedora and the big damp patches under his arms. He told her he could not report the black man to Judge Whidden, but neither could he disregard the theft.

"Why the hell not?" Alice said. In her outrage, she felt violated and seemed willing to do either one. "These rednecks like our money but they don't like us, and boy, it's mutual," she said, voice rising. "I want to get out of this damned place!"

NEXT MORNING, he was itchy-eyed from lack of sleep and felt disorganized and indecisive. "I just don't think we can go around accusing people," he complained.

"Who's asking you to accuse anybody? Whose tape deck was it, anyway? Forget it!"

"Maybe it *was* my fault, getting him drunk. Maybe he set it down someplace, forgot about it."

"Keep talking, pal. You know he took it, and you know you're not going to report him, and he knows it, too. So let's get out of here."

"Alice, we just can't pretend it never happened, that's all!"

"Why not? Why the hell *not*?"

He was surprised by her set, cold expression. She rolled over in bed and would not look at him. He wanted to shout at her, something like "Because we're *citizens*!," but he was wary of her tongue, and did not dare. "Look," he said, "we'll face him with it, tell him how crazy he is to try something like this. We'll talk to him out in the boat."

"*You* talk to him. Talk to him man to man. Straight from the shoulder." She shrugged him away when he reached down to her. "I'm staying here."

GIVING DICKIE AS MUCH ROOM as possible, he sat in the bow, and even from here he could smell the rum on him. He had only to look at the curled lip under the hat, the deep brow creases, the drinker's simmering belligerence and crazed hauteur, to know that Dickie was awaiting him. The black man did not whistle, scarcely seemed to breathe, and his sculling oar probed so softly through the water that only the wan motions of the bottom life gave evidence of their gloomy voyage across the waste.

In his anger at Alice, he had forgotten the sunburn cream, and the bright windy morning sun punished his sore places, but for once the guide worked hard to find a snook. In hidden channels Burkett cast where the long finger pointed. No fish rose. Then Dickie, speaking for the first time that morning, whispered, "Dat place. Try'm again," and Burkett dropped his lure in a brown eddy where the mangrove branches, dragged by currents, bowed and beckoned.

The earth responded with a hard thump on his line, which veered out sideways from the skiff, slitting the water, then shot back toward the channel. As Burkett hollered, a flashing brown-and-silver fish leapt from the tide, shaking sun-shined drops of water from its gills. It smacked the surface, bringing the water and green leaves to life.

Dickie was already turning toward it, moving skillfully and fast, before Burkett yelped at him to swing the boat. The fish was stripping too much of the light line, and he worked it carefully. Minutes later, when the lean, strong thing lay gasping on the boards between them, he reached down gently and touched it. "Snook," he marveled. "How about that? *Snewk!*" He burst out laughing. "Fisher Woman! Wait till she sees *this*!"

155

Dickie produced a curdled smile of pride, and his eye held for the first time all day. When Burkett said, "Too bad we don't have that rum along, to celebrate," Dickie was ready.

"Yassuh, we's got it, suh." Dickie whisked the bottle out from beneath the seat and thrust it at Burkett in a kind of challenge. "Got lef' dere yest'day," Dickie said, although most of it was gone.

Burkett saw that Dickie knew that Burkett knew Dickie was lying. He grinned in exhilaration and relief, waiting for Dickie to produce the tape deck, too. Instead, Dickie offered a dirty plastic glass, and Burkett poured himself a drink, handing back the rum. The guide finished it with a loud gasp and hurled the bottle violently into the mangroves.

"Dickie, I wonder . . ." But the man's head was already shaking, as if loose on a broken neck. "The tape deck," Burkett finished quickly, to make the premature denial less preposterous. The man hid behind a wild-eyed darkie mask, and rolled his eyes.

"Nawsuh, nawsuh, ain't seen nothin, nawsuh!"

Dickie veered out over the water on his pole, turning the skiff, feet twisting on the worn green paint, black veins ropy beneath dull black hide strangely silvered by sun-dried salt water.

"I don't want to get anyone in trouble," Burkett said after a moment, striking match upon wet match and sucking foolishly on the damp cigarette. "I'd rather not report this to Mr. Whidden."

Dickie's head only shook more violently, as if trying to escape the cords in his straining neck. "Nawsuh, doan go jitterin Judge Jim!" He started to say something else, then stopped.

"You have to trust me," Burkett said, awaiting him, but Dickie would not meet his eye. He muttered hopelessly, "Bes' fish dat same spot, you gone get de next one."

Burkett shook his head. "We're going in," he said, with as much menace as he could muster. Dark rain clouds off the Gulf shrouded the sun, which had burned him badly. He turned his back and laid his rod down in the boat.

The frightened guide was muttering to himself, and Burkett thought, I don't know how to help him. Not until they arrived at the main channel, and the royal palms and roofs came into view, did he turn to confront Dickie a last time. Before he could speak, Dickie howled in anguish, "Why you come roun' here causin trouble! Everythin goin *good* befo' you come!"

At opposite ends of the boat, they averted their faces and were silent. The last recourse was to threaten Dickie with a public accusation, but he doubted his own will to carry it through. At the expense of a small tape deck and some minor irritation, how much easier it would have been to forget the goddamned "principle of the thing." He was defeated. Alice is right, he thought, we'll go on home.

Judge Jim Whidden awaited them on shore. With the wide-eyed calm of a prey creature, the guide observed the line of white people as he eased the skiff up to the dock. And the people, too, were calm, their collective visage withdrawn, noncommittal.

"Git that boat on in here, Dickie," the Judge ordered, although the prow already nudged the pilings. Dickie flipped the snook onto the dock, and Burkett followed.

The Judge laid a heavy arm across his shoulders. "Tape toy, ain't it? Well, you don't wanta worry, Lawyer, I already got a purty good idea about it, a purty damn good idea. I got goin on it soon's they told me your missus was

157

huntin around the premises for somethin. But you oughta had reported it this mornin."

Burkett nodded submissively, and later he remembered this with shame. He longed to dismiss this big man coldly, but the man and the throng behind the man were overpowering. And after all, what harm had this "judge" done? Hadn't he been friendly and solicitous? And wasn't he sincere in his outrage now?

Judge Jim told Dickie to go straight to his office, then led Burkett toward his cabin as if he were taking him behind the woodshed, a big bad boy in shorts caught with a snook. "I got a purty good idea," he muttered, sucking his teeth by way of savoring his own deductive powers. "Not in *my* town! Not in *my* motel they don't rob the tourists, no sir!"

"They?" Burkett's voice sounded too high to him. His red nose and forehead, the red knees and shins, were swollen dry, and he felt a little dizzy, and he heard the nervousness in his own laugh.

Judge Jim laughed with him, very briefly. "That's a hot one, ain't it?" He chuckled without pleasure. "You're keeping up your sense of humor, boy." The voice had a new quality, as if the stranger had stumbled and exposed a weakness. There was no mistaking a proprietary tightening of the fingers above Burkett's elbow.

"There's something we have to get straight—" Burkett stopped short, twisting his arm free. "I don't want anyone accused of theft, it's just not worth it!"

"Now hold on, Lawyer!" Whidden reared back a little, squinted. "Nobody's gonna accuse nobody, just ask 'em a few questions. That's my bounden duty, ain't it? I just can't let 'em think, not for one damn minute—"

"Let *who* think?"

"There you go again, Lawyer!" Judge Jim shook his head and smiled. "I got my eye on the white trash, too, and we got our share of it, believe you me. Nobody's sayin a man's okay just cause he's white, you know. I ain't sayin that." He paused for emphasis. "Now Johnny, that's the yard man, and Aunt Tattie, that tidies up the cabins, and Dickie there, they all good niggers far as I know, and I knowed 'em all my life. But hell, boy, it just stands to reason! I mean, how many *white* people you seen around your room?"

"I'd just rather forget the whole business, if it's all right with you."

For a moment, Judge Whidden considered Burkett's pale legs, the baggy shorts, red shins, the torn wet sneakers.

"It ain't," he said.

Judge Jim took Burkett's arm again, concerned, cajoling. "I mean, you're down here to try out our fishin, ain't that right, you and the missus, you want to have yourself a dandy time? And how can I show folks a dandy time when their personal propitty ain't safe, even?" He patted the other's shoulder, then swung away along the white shell path toward his office.

"But you have no *authority* to make arrests—"

Judge Jim turned to look him over. "Don't think so, Lawyer? Sheriff ain't no further than my phone, and he don't ask questions. Not here he don't." He came back and thrust out a big hand, taking the fish away as Burkett flinched.

"I'll take care of that for you," he said. "Just go on in and chew the fat with your little lady. You all just enjoy yourselves, y'hear? Got a vespers and bingo over to the church this evenin, everyone welcome. First Baptist

159

Church." He was smiling again, but the smile had jelled. "Bet you people never knowed today was Sunday."

Burkett watched him go. He told himself he was too old for shorts, he would never wear these stupid shorts again.

Alice was watching through the window. "I went over to the café," she whispered, close to tears. "I thought about what you said about not accusing people, and I wondered if maybe he left it there last night, when he was drunk. I didn't mention him!" she added hastily, seeing his expression. "I asked if maybe *you* had left it there."

He said nothing. Going inside, he saw that she had packed their bags.

BECAUSE HE WOULD NOT leave that afternoon ("You got your damned snipe, didn't you!?"), they fought. At first she said she admired his attitude and was ashamed that she had lost her nerve, but when she realized he meant to see it through, she jeered at his stupid principles and stupid inability to mind his own business that had caused all the trouble in the first place. He got angry, too, dismissing her as the usual fair-weather liberal, the kind that always quit when the going got rough.

In the dead aftermath, he had drunk most of the whiskey, and later, an indefinite time later, he lay sweating in bed, heart pounding from a dream about night creatures from the open sea drifting over the white flats like moon shadows. A frightened voice tore at the dream—*Get out of here, goddamn you! Go away!* He turned on his back and saw his wife's silhouette against the window. A big voice came from across the yard:

"Goddamnit, nigger, you sit tight till I git my pants on!"

She leaned across and clenched his arm. "I heard someone

outside fooling around, right by our porch! I yelled at him!" Outside the window, a few yards from the porch door, a black man stood still as a rabbit against the hot white moonlight of the yard, and a screen door banged.

Burkett lay silent a long moment, listening. Then he sat up. "Goddamnit, Alice." He brushed away her plea. His palms were wet. He got out of bed, stumbling a little. "Goddamnit, Alice." He repeated it under his breath, then said it aloud again, stupidly, wiping his palms on his pajama legs, trying in vain to concentrate on his wife, who was weeping quietly. He thought, Now why can't she shut up? He longed to strike away her voice, all the damned voices.

The last shreds of the dream had blown away and still there was that moaning in the yard. He groped after his clothes, shaking her off. "Oh Christ!" she cried. "Let *them* fight it out! You just stay out of it!" When he stepped onto the screened porch, the moaning stopped.

Demanding something, Whidden was cuffing the small black man, who was on his knees. The Judge still had him by the collar and was yanking him back and forth with short piston strokes of his thick arm, both bodies black against the sand.

"Ain't your business," Whidden told Burkett without looking at him. "Go on back to bed."

Voices from the street drifted quietly into the yard.

"Sound like a stuck hawg, don't it? Hear him all the way down to the dock."

"What's that nigger doin here, middle of the night?"

"Better find out, ain't we?"

"That's what I'm doin," Whidden said. "You boys go home."

"Who's that standin in the shadders? That the federal?" 161

Burkett stepped into the yard.

"That there's my tourist, Speck. The one got stole off of."

No one moved. Burkett listened to the frightened moaning of the black man, who lay crumpled where Whidden had shoved him away, and the rasp of Whidden, breathing hard from his exertions, and the crazy ring of crickets, louder and louder.

"Heard you was interested in shrimp boats, mister." The voice was quiet. "Take you out night fishin in the Gulf, you so damn interested. Take your wife, too."

This slow hard voice spoke straight into his ear. On the soft sand, as silent as a ray, the man had eased up to a point just behind his shoulder.

Burkett stood still. He did not turn to look. He said, "Thanks." He said, "We have to leave tomorrow." Later he recalled having glanced at Whidden, as if seeking protection from the law. Hands on hips, the Judge studied the ground, like a man thinking something through.

Then Alice's hand was tugging at his pajama top, and Burkett backed into the cabin as that slow voice said, "Gonna miss the lynchin, then," and the others laughed. Alice clutched at him, and he put his hand over her mouth.

Through thin curtains, he watched thin men convene around the Judge. Hands in hip pockets, all but Whidden were looking at the door where he had gone. They were laughing so quietly he could scarcely hear them. He saw the moon glint on a tooth and thought about a ring of panting dogs.

Then someone spat on the white sand, and the crickets started up again, one by one around the moonlit yard. The Judge spat, too, and turned toward the café. "Lock him in the shed, there, Speck. I'll get onto it first thing in the mornin."

The man in the white Sunday shirt prodded the yard man with his boot.

"Let's move it, Johnny."

Burkett could not sleep. Going over the sequence of events, he realized it could have been Johnny after all.

At first light he got up and dressed, ignoring Alice, and crossed the dirty footprints in the sand to the rear door of the café. When nobody answered his soft knock, he sat on the porch steps in the dawn grayness, trying to clear his head.

An ancient bus came down the street and several black people got out, Dickie among them. Dickie unlocked the café door, and Burkett entered behind him. Shoulders high, eyes glaring, Dickie looked puffed up with threat like a huge bird. "Judge Jim ain' b'lievin *nobody* who go 'cusin Dickie! Jes' cause de man *white*? You crazy, mistuh!"

Burkett heard the Judge's voice. He trailed it into a back room, where Whidden was drinking coffee with the man Speck. The Judge waved his guest to an empty seat, shouting at Dickie to hurry it up with the Lawyer's coffee, then turned in his wood swivel chair and leaned back, grinning.

"Rode my tourist here kinda hard last night, now di'nt you, Speck?"

Speck returned Burkett's gaze without expression. "Made him homesick, ah guess."

"Ol' Speck never meant no harm, no harm at all!" Laughing, Judge Whidden slapped Burkett's arm with the back of his hand. "See, Speck don't rightly come from around here. Come up on them night fishin boats from Frigate Key. To hear ol' Speck let on sometimes, they's got

163

better fishin down to Frigate Key than we do here!" Judge Jim leaned over and took a noisy swallow from his coffee.

"Mr. Whidden, we're not pressing any charges!"

"Why, that's all right. We'll press 'em by ourselves."

When Whidden put his hands behind his head, still chuckling, Burkett struggled to control his voice. "Look," he said, "you have no authority. I'm not leaving here without talking to the Sheriff—"

"Why, sure you are!" In sudden anger, Judge Jim shouted, banging his chair down hard. "*Sure* you are, boy! That's *just* what you're going to do!" He folded his arms across his chest, nodding his head. Then he smiled again. "Soon's you pay up, of course." Burkett was still staring at him, and he said comfortably, "You told us last night you was leavin, so I give up your room."

"Between midnight and this morning?"

"Yessir, between midnight and this mornin." Whidden was trying not to laugh. "Yessir, I give that room up to ol' Speck here. Speck been needin a room in the worst way, ain't that right, Speck?"

Dickie's head appeared out of the corridor. Looking at the wall, he said, "How he want dat coffee?"

"Lawyer likes it integrated, ain't that right, Lawyer?" Judge Jim sighed. "Dickie, c'mere a minute." Contemplating the Lawyer, the Judge placed his fingertips with light restraint on Dickie's forearm.

Dickie was staring blindly in the general direction of the splayed white woman on the girlie calendar over Whidden's head, and noticing this, Speck sat up slowly, stiff as a bird dog. "Hey nigger," he said in a flat voice. Dickie jerked his head so that it stared sideways, out the window, and Whidden's grip tightened.

"Lawyer Burkett don't care none for no 'Hey nigger,'
Speck. Round here, we're integrated good. We say, 'Hey
Nigra!'"

The Judge sighed, squinting up at his guest.

"While back I told you I was gettin goin on this, right?
So what I done, I got Dickie in here, and I told him I di'nt
much care who done it, him or Johnny, but less I find out
quick, it was gonna be hard time for both, and that's the
road gang. So Dickie been tellin me that Johnny got hisself
some kind of a Injun woman out in the cypress, that right,
Dickie?" The Judge cocked his head back, speaking to
Dickie over his shoulder. "Been hard up for money, that
right, Dickie?" Chuckling, he let Dickie go, and the black
man fled the room.

"So he says Johnny did it."

"Well, he di'nt exactly *say* that, Lawyer, cause he don't
exactly know, but after last night we can sure as hell agree
that Johnny knows something about *somethin*. I'm gonna
get that son'bitch in here in a minute, and he's gonna tell
ol' Speck and me just what he done with your little tape
toy."

"I'll be back in a minute," Burkett said.

Dickie, coming with his coffee, backed up into the
kitchen. He seemed astonished by the anger in Burkett's
face.

"Goddamnit, you go get that tape deck."

"Johnny took it! Took it home dat night! Got scairt, dass
all, he was bringin it back, den Miz Alice hollers out and
Judge Jim caught'm!" Seeing Burkett's doubt, he went on
furiously, "Tellin you God's truth! Maybe Johnny slung it
into de bush someplace! Doan know *where* he got it!"

"Well, go find out! He's over in the shed!" He shook

Dickie's arm, slopping the coffee. "Suppose he tells that man in there who gave it to him in the first place?" Dickie just stared at him. "Christ, what does it *matter* now who took it? You're *both* in trouble!"

Aware of a furious impulse to cuff Dickie, to yell at him in exasperation—*Stupid damn nigger!*—Burkett was suddenly all out of breath. He went outside and sat down heavily on the stoop. There would be no victory here, whatever happened. Dickie came slowly to the screen door.

"Just *get* it, that's all! I'll say I found it!" Once again the guide was hissing his denials through the sagging screen, but the hissing faltered. Burkett could hear the rusty doorknob turning, forth and back and forth again.

"Better trust me," he said. "I'm the best you've got." Still the man stood there. Then he snaked through the door and down the steps and around the building, his hands spread-fingered in conflicting agonies.

Burkett walked up the street a little way, trying to calm himself, as the sun rose to the black tops of the eastern trees. The palm fronds shivered hard as the wind freshened. In the early light, the water of the creek was thick bronze silver, like a heavy oil.

Alice came running. He turned his back to her in sign that she must not interfere and returned to the kitchen door, where a paper bag was sitting on the steps.

She looked exhausted. "Dickie took that bag just now from beneath our porch!" Her voice rang loudly in the stillness, and his nerves gave way. He snapped at her, "Just stay out of the way!" Her face was crumbling as he mounted the steps, but he could not deal with it, not now.

Poking his head into the kitchen, he said to Dickie, "How much do I owe you? For guiding, I mean?"

"You's gots to see Judge Jim 'bout dat."

He took a deep breath and knocked. "Judge Jim?" He entered the back room. "I'm sorry for all the trouble," he began, holding out the small thing in both hands, like an offering.

"Oh Godawmighty!" Whidden said, half-rising from his chair, wiping spat coffee from his chin with the back of his hand. "What in hell is goin on around this place!"

When Burkett produced his traveler's checks and began to sign them, Whidden sank back slowly, both hands flat down on his desk, trying to control himself. "You ain't so smart as you think you are," he muttered finally, counting the checks. "This business ain't finished by a long shot."

He raised his eyes. "What you waitin on, Lawyer? You people get the hell out of my town."

Passing the kitchen, Burkett thanked Dickie, offering his hand. The black man backed away. In a stifled voice he said, "You leavin here. Leavin us stuck wit it."

Burkett thought, I'm stuck with it, too.

To the east, the royal palms on the old street were black against the growing sky. In front of their cabin, Alice was waiting in the car, her pale face watching out for him over her shoulder. He had hardly started across the yard when Whidden's voice bawled, "You, goddamnit, Dickie, get on in here!"

"Keep movin," Speck called quietly, when Burkett faltered.

1985

LUMUMBA
LIVES

1

HE COMES BY TRAIN out of the wilderness of cities, he
has come from abroad this very day. At mid-life he has
returned to a hometown where he knows no one.

The train tugs softly, slides away, no iron jolt and bang
as in his childhood, no buck and yank of couplings, only
a gathering clickety-click away along the glinting track,
away along the river woods, the dull shine of the water,
north and away toward the great bend in the Hudson.

Looking north, he thinks, The river has lost color. The
track is empty, the soft late summer sunshine fills the bend,
the day is isolate.

HE IS THE ONE PASSENGER left on the platform, exposed to the bare windows of Arcadia. He might be the one
survivor of a cataclysm, emerging into the flat sun of the
river street at the foot of this steep decrepit town fetched

up against the railroad tracks on the east slope of the Hudson River Valley. What he hasn't remembered in the years he has been gone is the hard bad colors of its houses, the dirtied brick and fire bruises of the abandoned factory, the unbeloved dogs, the emptiness.

On this railroad street, a solitary figure with a suitcase might attract attention. To show that his business is forthright, he crosses the old cobbles quickly to the salesmen's hotel at the bottom of the downhill slide of human habitation. The dependent saloon has a boarded-up side door marked "Ladies Entrance," and the lobby reminds him, not agreeably, of looted colonial hotels in the new Africa that he supposes he will never see again.

THE STRANGER'S SOFT VOICE and quiet suit, his discreet manner, excite the suspicion of the clerk, who puts down a mop to shuffle behind the desk and slap out a registration form. This dog-eared old man spies on the name as it is being written. "We got a park here by that name," he says.

The man shakes his head as if shaking off the question. Asked where he's from, he says he has lived abroad. The foreign service. Africa.

"Africa," the clerk says, licking a forefinger and flicking the sports pages of a New York daily. "You'll feel right at home, then." He reads a while as if anticipating protest. "Goddam Afros overflowing right out of the city. Come up this way from Yonkers, come up at night along the river."

Nodding at his own words, the clerk looks up. "You have a wife?"

"I saw them," the stranger says. At Spuyten Duyvil, where the tracks emerged from the East River and turned north up the Hudson, black men had watched his train from

169

the track sidings. "They were fishing," he says.

The stranger's fingertips lie flat upon the counter as if he meant to spring into the air. He is a well-made man of early middle age and good appearance, controlled and quiet in his movements. Dry blond hair is combed across a sun-scarred bald spot.

"Fishing," the clerk says, shaking his head. "I guess you learned to like 'em over there."

The man says nothing. He has shallow and excited eyes. He awaits his key.

Irritable and jittery under that gaze, the clerk picks out a key with yellowed fingers. "How many nights?"

The man shrugs. Asked if he wishes to see the room, he shrugs again. He will see it soon enough. When he produces a thick roll of bills to pay the cash deposit in advance, the old man inspects the bills, lip curled, checking the stranger's face at the same time. Still holding the cash as if in evidence, he leans over the desk to glare at the large old-fashioned leather suitcase.

The stranger says, "I'll take it up. It's heavy."

"I'll bet," says the clerk, shaking his head over the weight he had almost been asked to hump up the steep stair.

On the floor above, the man listens a moment, wondering briefly why he sets people on edge even before trouble occurs. Their eyes reflect the distemper he is feeling.

He opens, closes, bolts the transomed door.

THE ROOM IS PENITENTIAL, it is high-ceilinged and skinny, with defunct fire pipes, no pictures, a cold-water sink, a scrawny radiator, a ruined mirror on the wall. The water-marked walls are the color of blue milk. The bedside table is so small that there is no room for a lamp. The

Gideon Bible sits in the chipped washbasin. A rococo ceiling fixture overhead, a heavy dark armoire, an iron bed with a stained spread of slick green nylon.

The pieces stand in stiff relation, like spare mourners at a funeral whom no one is concerned to introduce.

His reflected face in the pocked mirror is unforgiving. The room has no telephone, and there will be no visitors. He has no contacts in this place, which is as it should be. Checking carefully for surveillance devices, he realizes the precaution is absurd, desists, feels incomplete, finishes anyway.

Big lonesome autumn flies buzz on the windowsill. The high bare window overlooks the street, the empty railroad station, the river with its sour burden of industrial filth carried down from bleak ruined upstate valleys. Across the river the dark cliffs of the Palisades wall off the sky.

HIS MOTHER had not felt well enough to see him off, nor had his father driven him down to the station. The Assistant Secretary for African Affairs had wished to walk his English setter, and had walked his son while he was at it.

We want you to gain the Prime Minister's confidence. He may trust you simply because you are my son.

Unfortunately the more . . . boyish? . . . elements in our government want another sort of prime minister entirely. They are sure to find some brutal flunky who, for a price, will protect our business interests.

The Assistant Secretary had not waited for the train.

Make the most of this opportunity, young man.

By which he meant, *You have this chance to redeem yourself, thanks to my influence.*

171

The gardener had brought the leather suitcase. From the empty platform they watched his father stride away. At the north end of the street, the tall straight figure passed through the iron gate into the park.

The gardener cried, *So it's off to Africa ye are! And what will ye be findin there, I'm askin?*

Turning from the window, he removes his jacket, drapes it on a chair; he does not remove the shoulder holster, which is empty. He contemplates the Assistant Secretary's ancient suitcase as if the solution to his life were bundled up in it.

He unpacks his clothes, takes out a slim chain, locks and binds the suitcase, chains it to the radiator.

On the bed edge he sits upright for a long time as if expecting something. He has trained himself to wait immobile hour after hour, like a sniper, like a roadside African, like a poised hawk, ready for its chance, thinking of nothing.

A dying fly comes to his face. It wanders. Its touch is weak and damp. He does not brush it away.

By the river at the north end of town is a public park established by his grandfather, at one time a part of the old Harkness estate. His father's great-uncle, in the nineteenth century, had bought a large tract of valleyside and constructed a great ark of a house with an uplifting view of the magnificent Palisades across the river, and his descendants had built lesser houses in the park, in one of which, as an only child, he had spent the first years of his life.

Not wishing to hurry, he does not go there on the first day, contenting himself with climbing the uphill street and buying a new address book. He must make sure that each day has its errand, that there is a point to every day, day after day.

The real-estate agent, a big man with silver hair slicked hard and puffy dimpled chin, concludes that the old Harkness property will have just the "estate" that Mr. . . .? might be looking for.

"Call me Ed," the agent says, sticking out his hand. The client shakes it after a brief pause but does not offer his name.

All but the river park presented to the village was sold off for development, the agent explains, when the last Harkness moved away some years before. But the big trees and the big stone houses—the "manor houses," the agent calls them—are still there, lending "class" to the growing neighborhood.

Mother says you are obliged to sell the house. I'd like to buy it.
Absolutely not!

THE NARROW ROAD between high ivied walls was formerly the service driveway, and the property the realtor has in mind is the gardener's brick cottage, which shares the river prospect with "the big house" on the south side of an old stand of oak and hickory.

As a child he fled his grandmother's cambric tea to take refuge in this cottage full of cooking smells. His nurse was married to the gardener, and he knows at once that he will buy the cottage even if the price is quite unreasonable. So gleeful is he in this harmony of fate that his fingers work in his coat pockets.

He has no wish to see the rooms until all intervening life   173 has been cleaned out of them. Before the agent can locate the keys, he says, "I'll take it."

When the agent protests—"You don't want to look inside?"—he counts off five thousand dollars as a deposit and walks back to the car, slipping into the passenger seat, shutting the door.

Not daring to count or pocket so much cash, the agent touches the magic bricks in disbelief. He pats the house as he might pat a horse and stands back proudly. "Nosir, they don't make 'em like this, not anymore."

The one thing missing here is burglar lights, the agent says—a popular precaution these days, he assures his client, climbing back into the car. Like the man at the hotel, he evokes the human swarm emerging from the slums and coming up along the river woods at night. "Engage in criminal activity," he emphasizes when the other man, by his silence, seems to question this.

"Ready to go?" the client says, looking out the window.

On the way home he inquires about New York State law in regard to shooting burglars, and the agent laughs. "Depends on his color," he says, and nudges his client, and wishes he had not. "Don't get me wrong," he says.

Back at the office the agent obtains the buyer's name to prepare the contract. "You've come to the right place, all right! Any relation?"

The man from Africa ignores the question. He will reveal that he belongs here in his own good time. First he wants everything to be in place, the little house, its furnishings, his history. The place will be redone in the style of the big house across the hedge, with English wallpapers, old walnut furniture, big thick towels and linen sheets, crystal and porcelain, such as his parents might have left him,

174

setting off the few good pieces he had put in storage after their deaths. The inside walls will be painted ivory, as the house was, and the atmosphere will be sunny and cheerful, with an aura of fresh mornings in the spring.

Once the cottage is ready, his new life will commence, and the names of new friends will flower in his address book.

TO HIS CHILDHOOD HOUSE he wishes to return alone, on foot. Since he means to break in, he makes sure that he leaves the hotel unobserved, that he is not followed. Not that there is anyone to follow him, it is simply a good habit, sound procedure.

He enters the park by the iron gate beyond the railroad station, climbing transversely across a field, then skirting an old boxwood border so as not to be seen by the unknown people who have taken over his uncle's house. He trusts the feel of things and not his sight, for nothing about this shrunken house looks quite familiar. It was always a formal, remote house, steep-roofed and angular, but now it has the dark of rottenness, of waterlogged wood.

He hurries on, descending past the stables (no longer appended to his uncle's house or frequented by horses, to judge from the trim suburban cars parked at the front). In the old pines stands a grotesque disc of the sort recommended to him by his would-be friend the agent, drawing a phantasmagoria of color from the heavens.

He is seeking a childhood path down through the wood, across the brook, and uphill through the meadow.

FROM THE TREES come whacks and pounding, human cries. A paddle-tennis court has spoiled the brook, which is

175

now no more than an old shadow line of rocks and broken brush. Wary of his abrupt appearance, his unplayful air—or perhaps of a stranger not in country togs, wearing unsuitable shoes for a country weekend—the players challenge him. Can they be of help?

He says he is looking for the Harkness house.

"Who?" one man says.

Calling the name—*Harkness!*—through the trees, hearing his own name in his own voice, makes him feel vulnerable as well as foolish, and his voice is thickened by a flash of anger. He thinks, I have lost my life while soft and sheltered men like these dance at their tennis.

He manages a sort of smile, which fails to reassure them. They look at each other, they look back at him. They do not resume playing.

"Harkness," one man says finally, cocking his head. "That was long ago. My grandfather knew your father. Something like that."

Dammit, he thinks. Who said that was my name!

Now the players bat the ball, rally a little. He knows they watch him as he skirts the court and leaves the trees and climbs the lawn toward the stone house set against the hillside at the ridge top.

His father's house has a flagstone terrace with a broad prospect of the Hudson. It is a good-sized stone house, with large cellar rooms, a downstairs, upstairs, and a third story with servants' rooms and attic. Yet even more than his uncle's place it seems diminished since his childhood. Only the great red oak at this south end of the house seems the right size, which confuses him until he realizes that in the decades he has been away it has grown larger.

In a snapshot of himself beneath this tree, in baggy shorts, he brandishes a green garden stake shoved through the hole of a small flower pot, used as a hand guard. He is challenging to a duel the Great Dane, Inga.

The oak stands outside the old "sun room," with its player piano and long boxes of keyed scrolls, and a bare parquet floor for children's games and tea dancing. The world has changed since a private house had a room designed for sun and dancing.

The weather-greened cannon are gone from the front circle. Once this staid house stood alone, but now low dwellings can be seen, crowding forward like voyeurs through what is left of the thin woods farther uphill.

Completing the circuit of the house, he arrives at the formal garden—"the autumn garden," his mother called it, with its brick wall and flowered gate, its view down across the lawn to the woods and river. The garden is neglected, gone to weeds. Though most are fallen, his mother's little faded signs that identified the herb species still peep from a coarse growth of goldenrod, late summer asters.

In other days, running away, he had hidden past the dusk in the autumn garden, peering out at the oncoming dark, waiting for a voice to call him into the warm house. They knew his ways, and no one ever called. Choked with self-pity, a dull yearning in his chest, he would sneak up the back stairs without his supper.

The boiler room has an outside entrance under the broad terrace, on the downhill side. He draws on gloves to remove a pane, lever the lock. He crosses the spider-shrouded light to the cellar stair and enters the cold house from below, turning the latch at the top of the stair, edging the door open to listen. He steps into the hall. The house feels hollow, and white sheets hide the unsold furniture. In the

177

kitchen he surprises an old cockroach, which scuttles beneath the pipes under the sink.

THE SILENCE FOLLOWS HIM around the rooms. On his last visit before his father sold the house, faint grease spots still shone through the new paint on the ceiling of his former bedroom. Sometimes, sent up to his room for supper, he had used a banged spoon as catapult to stick the ceiling with rolled butter pats and peanut-butter balls.

From his parents' bedroom, from the naked windows, he gazes down over the lawn, standing back a little to make sure he is unseen. The court is empty. He is still annoyed that the paddle-tennis players have his name. Possibly they are calling the police. To be arrested would reflect badly on his judgment, just when he has asked if there might be an assignment for him someplace else.

HEARING A CAR, he slips downstairs and out through the cellar doors.

"Looking for somebody?"

The caretaker stands in the service driveway by the corner of the house. He wears a muscle-tight black T-shirt and big sideburns. He is wary, set for trouble, for he comes no closer.

Had this man seen him leave the house?

He holds the man's eye, keeping both hands in his coat pockets, standing motionless, dead silent, until uneasiness seeps into the man's face.

"I got a call. The party said there was somebody lookin for someone."

"Can't help you, I'm afraid." Casually he shrugs and keeps on going, down across the lawn toward the brook.

"Never seen them signs?" the man calls after him, when

the stranger is a safe distance away. "What do you want around here, mister?"

2

WITH SOME IDEA of returning to the hotel by walking south beside the tracks, he makes his way down along the brook, his street shoes slipping on the aqueous green and sunshined leaves.

Whenever, in Africa, he thought of home, what he recalled most clearly was this brook below the house and a sandy eddy where the idle flow was slowed by his rock dam. Below this pool, the brook descended through dark river woods to a culvert that ran beneath the tracks into the Hudson. Lit by a swift sun that passed over the trees, the water crossed the golden sand—the long green hair twined on slowly throbbing stems, the clean frogs and quick fishes and striped ribbon snakes—the flow so clear that the diadem of a water skater's shadow would be etched on the sunny sand glinting below. One morning a snake seized a small frog—still a tadpole, really, a queer thing with new-sprouted legs and a thick tail—and swallowed it with awful gulps of its unhinged jaws. Another day, another year, perhaps, peering into the turmoil in a puff of sunlit sand of the stream bottom, he saw a minnow in the mouth and claws of a mud-colored dragon. The dragonfly nymph loomed in his dreams for years thereafter, and he hated the light-filled creature it became, the crazy sizzle of the dragonfly's glass wings, the unnatural hardness of this thing when it struck the skin.

For hours he would hunch upon a rock, knees to his ears, staring at the passages and deaths. Sometimes he thought he would like to study animals. How remote this dark brook was from the Smiling Pool in his Peter Rabbit book up in   179 the nursery, a meadow pool all set about with daffodils and roses, birds, fat bumblebees, where mirthful frogs, fun-loving fish, and philosophical turtles fulfilled their life on earth without a care.

Even then he knew that Peter Rabbit was a mock-up of the world, meant to fool children.

NEARING THE RAILROAD, the old brook trickles free from the detritus, but the flow is a mere seepage, draining into a black pool filled with oil drums. An ancient car, glass-shattered, rust-colored, squats low in the thick Indian summer undergrowth where once—or so his father said—an Algonkin band had lived in a log village.

In the sun and silence of the river, he sits on the warm trunk of a fallen willow, pulling mean burrs from his city trousers. From here he can see across the tracks to the water and the Palisades beyond. Perhaps, he thinks, those sugar-maple yellows and hot hickory reds along the cliffs wel-comed Henry Hudson, exploring upriver with the tide four centuries before, in the days when this gray flood—at that time blue—swirled with silver fishes.

Hudson's ship—or so his father always claimed—had an elephant chained on the foredeck, an imposing present for the anticipated Lord of the Indies. Turned back at last by the narrowing river from his quest for the Northwest Pas-sage, fed up with the task of gathering two hundred pounds of daily fodder for an animal that daily burdened the small foredeck with fifteen to twenty mighty shits—his father's word, in its stiff effort at camaraderie, had astonished and delighted him—Henry the Navigator had ordered the ele-phant set free in the environs of present-day Poughkeepsie.

180 Strewing its immense sign through the woods, blaring its

longing for baobab trees to the rigid pines, the great beast surely took its place in Algonkin legend.

Misreading his son's eager smile, his father checked himself, sighed crossly, and stood up. *A vigorous Anglo-Saxon term, not necessarily a dirty word to be leered and giggled at. You should have outgrown all that by now.* He left the room before the boy found words to undo such awful damage.

BEYOND THE MISTED TREES, upriver, lies Tarrytown— Had someone tarried there? his mother asked his father, purling demurely. Why his father smiled at this he did not know. From Tarrytown one might see across the water to the cliffs where Rip Van Winkle had slept for twenty years. As a child he imagined a deep warm cleft full of autumn light, sheltered from the northeast storms and northwest winds. He peers across the mile of water, as if that shelter high up in clean mountains were still there.

In the Indian summer mist the river prospect looks much as he remembered it—indeed, much as it had been portrayed by the Hudson River School of painters so admired by his maternal grandmother. *Atrocious painters, all of them,* his father said. The small landscape of this stretch of river— was that in the crate of family things he had in storage? How much he has lost track of, in those years away.

He places a penny on the railroad track.

He longs to reassemble things—well, not "things" so much as continuity, that was his mother's word. Her mother had been raised on the west banks of the Hudson, and she could recall, from her own childhood, her great-aunt relating how *her* grandmother had seen Alexander Hamilton sculling downriver one fine morning just below their house—"Good day, Mr. Hamilton!"—and how Mr.

181

Hamilton had never returned that day, having lost his life to a Mr. Burr in a duel at Weehawken.

His father loved this story, too, the more so because that reach of river cliff had changed so little in the centuries between. For both of them, the memory of Mr. Hamilton had an autumnal melancholy that reached far back across the nation's history, to the Founding Fathers.

It seemed he had not responded to it properly.

I suppose you find it merely quaint, his mother said.

AT ONE TIME he attended Sunday school here in Arcadia, and he thinks he will rejoin the Episcopal Church. On sunny Sundays in white shirt and sober suit he will find himself sustained and calmed by stained-glass windows and Bach organ preludes. Afterward he will return to the garden cottage with its antique furniture, blue flowers in white rooms, fine editions, rare music, and a stately dog thumping its tail on a warm rug. He envisions an esoteric text, a string quartet, a glass of sherry on a sunlit walnut table in the winter—his parents' tastes, he realizes, acquired tastes he is determined to acquire.

In this civilized setting, smoking a pipe, he will answer questions from young women about Africa, and the nature of Africans, and how to deal judiciously with these Afro-Americans, so-called. Those who imagine that Africans are inferior do not know Africans, he'll say. Africans have their own sort of intelligence, they are simply not interested in the same things we are. Once their nature is understood, he'll say, Africans are Africans, wherever you find them, never mind what these bleeding-hearts may tell you.

A TRAIN COMES from the north, clicketing by, no longer dull coal black, as in his childhood, but a tube of blue-and-silver cars, no light between. In his childhood he could make out faces, but with increased speed the human beings are pale blurs behind the glass, and nobody waves to the man on the dead tree by the railroad tracks.

The wind and buffet of the train, the sting of grit, intensify his sense of isolation. To his wave, the train responds with a shrill whistle that is only a signal to the station at Arcadia, a half mile south.

He gets up, stretching, hunts the penny. It glints at him among the cinders. Honest Abe, tarnished by commerce, has been wiped right off the copper, replaced by a fiery smooth shine.

Looking north and south, he picks his way across the tracks. The third rail—if such it is—is a sheathed cable between pairs of rails marked "Danger Zone 700 Volts." Has the voltage increased since his childhood? *If you so much as point at that third rail,* explained his mother, who worried about his solitary expeditions to the river, *you'll be electrocuted, like one of those ghastly criminals up at Sing-Sing!* He hesitates before he crosses, stepping over this rail higher than necessary.

The tracks nearest the river are abandoned, a waste of rusted rails and splintered oaken ties and hard dry weeds. Once across, he can see north to the broad bend where a shoulder of the Palisades juts out from the far shore into the Tappan Zee. A thick new bridge has been thrust across the water, cutting off the far blue northern mountains. In his childhood, a white steamer of the Hudson River Day Line might loom around that bend at any moment, or a barge of bright tomato-red being towed by a pea-green tug, both fresh as toys. His father would evoke the passage of Robert Fulton's steamship *Claremont,* and the river trade on this

183

slow concourse, flowing south out of the far blue mountains.

In his own lifetime—is this really true?—the river has changed from blue to a dead gray-brown, so thickened with inorganic silt that a boy would not see his own feet in the shallows. The real-estate agent, not a local man but full of local lore, asserts that the Atlantic salmon have vanished from the Hudson, and that the striped bass and shad are so contaminated by the poisons dumped into these waters by the corporations that people are prohibited from eating them. Only the blacks, says he, come out to fish for them, prowling the no-man's-land of tracks and cinders.

A grit beach between concrete slabs of an old embankment is scattered with worn tires. He wonders, as his father had, at the sheer number of these tires, brought by forces unknown so very far from the roads and highways and dumped in low woods and spoiled sullen waters all across America, as if, in the ruined wake of the course of empire, the tires had spun away in millions down the highways and rolled off the bridges into the rivers and down into deep swamps of their own accord.

But the horizon is oblivious, the clouds are white, the world rolls on. Under the cliffs, the bend is yellow in the glow of maples, and the faraway water, reflecting the autumn sky, is gold and blue. Soiled though they are, the shining woods and glinting water and the bright steel tracks, the high golden cliffs across the river, seem far more welcoming than the valley slope above, with its tight driveways, smelly cars, vigilant houses.

For a long time, by the riverside, he sits on a drift log worn smooth by the flood, withdrawn into the dream of Henry Hudson's clear blue river, of that old America off to the north toward the primeval mountains, off to the west under the shining sky.

3

The real-estate agent has persuaded him to come to dinner, to celebrate his move into the cottage, and a van has delivered a large crate containing what is left of the family things. On a journey home after his father's death, he had got rid of everything else, glad to have Arcadia behind him. But when his years in Africa were ended, and he was faced with a return to the United States, where he knew no one, this crate, in his imagination, had overflowed with almost everything from childhood. However, all he finds are a few small antiques that could not be sold quickly yet had seemed too valuable to abandon. There are also a few unaccountable small scraps—a baby-blue bathroom rug with faded bears, the Peter Rabbit book, the photograph of his duel with the Great Dane Inga.

His grandmother's riverscape is jammed in carelessly, its gold frame chipped. Wrapped around his father's Hardy reels and .410 Purdy shotgun is the Assistant Secretary's worn-out hunting jacket, the silver brandy flask still in the pocket, the hard brown canvas and scuffed corduroy irrevocably stained with gun oil, bird blood, and the drool of setter dogs.

The riverscape is hung over the mantel, with the Purdy on oak dowel pins beneath. He likes the feel of the quick gun, with its walnut stock and blue-black finish, its fine chasing. He will keep it loaded, as a precaution against looters and marauders. Agent Ed has advised him to emulate the plump homes of his neighbors, which are walleyed with burglar lights, atremble with alarms.

However, he hates all that night glare, he feels less protected than exposed. As soon as his pistol permit is restored—he concocts this plan over his evening whiskeys—he'll use a silencer to extinguish every burglar light in the whole neighborhood.

Why scare off marauders, he asks the agent's wife at supper, when the death of one burglar at the hands of a private citizen would do more to prevent crime than all the floodlights in Westchester County? He has said this for fun, to alarm this upstate couple. Poor Ed loves this dangerous talk, having no idea that his guest means it, and as for the hostess, the woman is agog, her eyes loom huge and round behind her spectacles.

"You're such a . . . well, a *disturbing* man!" she says.

"Disturbed *me* from the very first day I met him!" Ed cries jovially to soften his wife's inadvertent candor. "I suppose you're waiting for a new foreign service job?"

"There won't be one," he says abruptly, as if admitting this to himself for the first time.

He drinks the whiskey he has carried to the table. That these folks want a Harkness for a friend is all too plain. He picks up the wine, sips it, blinks, pulls his head back from it, sets his glass down again. "A bit sweet," he explains, when her stare questions him.

Ed jars the table and his face goes red with a resentment that he has avoided showing until now. "Well, shit," he says. "You're a damn snob," he says.

"Oh my." The woman does not take her round eyes off their guest.

Ed scrapes his chair back and goes to the front door and opens it. "We just thought you might be kind of lonely," Mrs. Ed mourns.

"Probably likes it that way," the agent says.

Things are awry again. Afraid of something, he takes a large swallow of wine and nods approvingly. "Not bad at all," he says, with a poor smile.

"It's not just the wine," the agent warns his wife. The woman has crossed her bare arms on her chest in the cold draft that wanders through the opened door.

"I was hoping you'd call me Henry," he says, drinking more wine. "Very nice," he says. She turns her face away, as if unable to look upon his desperation. "Forgive me," he says.

"Nosir," the voice says from the door. "Nosir, I don't think we will."

4

NOT WANTING HIS NEW HOUSE to be finished, leaving things undone, he takes long walks along suburban roads and drives. People stare to let him know they have their eye on him. Bad dogs run out. Even so, the walks are dull and pointless. More and more often he returns to the low river woods, the endless iron stretch of tracks, the silent river, flickered over by migrating swallows.

One day in October, he crosses the tracks and sits on a dock piling with twisted bolts, wrenched free by some upriver devastation. The piling's faint creosote smell brings back some childhood boat excursion, upriver through the locks of Lake Champlain.

The breeze is out of the northwest, and has an edge to it. With a fire-blackened scrap of siding, he scrapes out a shelter under the old pilings, partly hidden from the woods by the pale sumac saplings that struggle upward from the cinders.

187

In the early autumn afternoon, out of the wind, he is warmed by the westering sun across the river. If the beach litter were piled in front of him, he thinks, he would be unseen even from the water. Not that there is anyone to see him, it is just the sheltered feeling it would give him. The freighters headed up to Albany, the tugs and barges, an occasional fat white motor cruiser with its nylon Old Glory flying from the stern, pass too far offshore to be aware of a hat-shadowed face in a pile of flotsam.

He hunches down a little, squinting out between his knees.

He is safe and secret, sheltered from the world, just as he had been long ago in his tree houses and attic hideouts, in the spruce hollow in the corner behind the lode of packages under the Christmas tree, in warm nests in the high summer grass, peeping out at the Algonkin Indians. *Delawares,* his father said. *Algonkin is the language family.* In the daytime, at least, no one comes along the tracks. He has the river kingdom to himself. As to whether he is content, he does not know.

He has packed dry sherry in his father's silver flask, a sandwich, a hard apple, and also a new bleeding-heart account of modern politics in the former Belgian Congo. His name receives harsh passing mention. He thinks, To hell with it. I did what was asked of me. I did my duty. Having the courage to dirty one's hands, without glory and at great risk of ingratitude, may become one's higher duty to one's country, wasn't that true?

The trouble was, he had not liked Lumumba. He had wondered if the Prime Minister might be unstable. Lumumba's hostility toward Europeans flared and shuddered like a fire in the wind but never died. He ate distractedly in small brief fits, growing thinner and thinner. He was moody, loud, self-contradictory, he smoked too much hemp, he drank a lot, he took one woman after another despite his devotion to his wife, he could not stop talking or stand still.

WILD DUCKS PASS BY within gun range, flaring away from his little cove with hard quacks of alarm. He swings his arms as if holding a gun, and they crumple and fall in a downward arc as he follows through. Watching them fly onward, he feels an exhilaration tinged with loss that wild fowl still tried to migrate south along this shore of poisoned mud and rust and cinders. On a northeast wind, in rain, his hiding place would serve well as a duck blind, for in order to land into the wind the birds would hook around over the open water and come straight in to the gun.

More ducks appear farther upriver where the black stumps of an old dock jut from the surface. The long rust heads and silver-white bodies are magically unsullied in the somber water. There are five.

NEEDING SOMETHING to look forward to, he decides upon a sacramental hunt. A hunter's stiff whiskey by the fire, the wild-duck supper with wild rice, the red Bordeaux from his mother's old colonial crystal decanter—thus will he consecrate the return of the Harkness family to Arcadia. Since it will happen only once, he can't be bothered with decoys, waders, far less a retriever. The river is too swift and deep to wade in, and in the unlikely event that a duck falls, the current is bound to carry it ashore.

To acquire a license to kill ducks he goes to Yonkers, not wishing to excite local curiosity. It seems absurd to bother about a license for one bird, when to shoot on the railroad right-of-way will be illegal in the first place. He applies for

189

the permit for the same reason that he would feel obliged to retrieve and eat any bird he shot, rather than waste it. His father had been strict about licenses, bag limits, and using what one killed, even in the days when ducks were plentiful. To offend this code would violate the hunt ceremony in some way, make the supper pointless.

He has no proof of U.S. residence in the previous year—in the previous two decades, if it comes to that. He does not say this lest his very citizenship be challenged by the hostile young black woman, who says he will have to identify himself, submit proof of residence, proof of citizenship. But he has no driver's license or certificate of birth, and can't tell her that his passport has been confiscated.

"Next!"

As for the huge hunting license, it looks nothing like the duck-stamp badge his father had worn upon his fishing hat. The new license is worn on the back, to facilitate identification by the game warden. Though he knows it is foolish, he feels he is being tricked into the open. One might as well wear a bull's-eye on one's back.

"Next!"

Are the authorities suggesting, he inquires, that the duck hunter is stupid as well as lawless, that he will shoot over his limit and make off with his booty, yet neglect to remove this grotesque placard from his back?

"We ain't suggesting nothing. That's the law." She waves him aside.

It disconcerts him that the hunter behind him in the line is black.

"Move along please! Next!"

While stalling, he folds a twenty-dollar bill into his application form and eases it back across the counter, at the same time requesting her to be more careful how she speaks to him. Raising her eyebrows at his tone, then at the money, she heaves around as if to summon her superior, giving him a chance to withdraw the bill. He does so quickly, winking at the black hunter, asking this female if he really requires proof that he is an American—doesn't he look like one?

With the back of her hand, she brushes away his application form, which flutters to the floor.

"I could bust you, mister. You just watch your step."

She is already processing the next application.

"*Everybody* looks American," she is saying. "*I* look American. And you know what, mister?" She looks up at him. "I *am* American. More than you." She points at the incomplete form in his hand. "I ain't lived in Africa for half my life."

Please do not confuse your activities in Africa with the foreign service, far less true service to your country, less still an honorable career that would make you a credit to this family.

When he raised his eyes, his mother averted hers. He flipped his father's note back at her, in a kind of spasm. The letter struck her at the collarbone and fell into her lap. She looked down at it for a long moment, then picked it up between two fingers and set it on the table. Her eyes glistened.

You've changed so, Henry, dear. When you went off to war, you grew so hard. It wasn't your fault, of course. Seeing all those dreadful things—it's enough to confuse anyone, I'm sure!

Before he could protest, she had slipped away from him.

You were such a lonely boy. How I wish you'd found somebody. Or become a naturalist! she added brightly. *Animals are so much easier, aren't they?*

Inappropriately, she tried to smile, as if to soothe him. 191

We shall always love you, dear.

His rivals killed him! he insisted. *Mother?* He had wanted to seize her, to shake from her frail body some pledge of loyalty. *Patrice was the Soviets' little macaque!*

She opened her eyes wide in mock astonishment—*Patrice?*

And your little Mr. Mobutu, dear? The dictator? Whose macaque is he?

HE DECIDES he will need decoys after all. His father's hand-carved balsa ducks, close-etched with wild colors, had been rigged with cedar keels and fine-smelling tarred cod line and square lead anchors on which the line was wrapped, leaving just enough room in the open center so that line and weight fitted neatly over bill and head. But sturdy wood decoys are no longer available, or not, at least, in these seedy river towns.

What are offered instead are swollen plastic mallards, drake mallards only, with heads the dead green of zinc alloy and the rest a bad industrial brown fit to attract those mongrel ducks that inhabited the dirty waters of the city parks and the pilings of old river docks in Yonkers. By means of gaudy plastic twine that would cut the hands in winter weather, each duck is rigged to a scrap of pig iron, sure to drag in any sort of wind.

He cannot bring himself to acquire more than three (*Always set an odd number,* his father had said, *in case of a lone bird*), since he would not harbor such horrors in his house, and does not intend to hunt ever again. So irritated is he by wasting money on such rubbish that he feels justified in commandeering a rain parka in its slim packet and a box of shotgun shells while he is at it.

At the cottage he finds a burlap sack for carrying and concealing the decoys, the dismantled gun, the shells, and a thermos of coffee in its leather case. That evening, he rigs a treble-hooked surf-casting lure on a length of line—a makeshift retrieval gear of his own devising.

Within a few days comes a forecast of northeast wind, with rain. Since his days are his own—the one activity left to him, now that the house is finished, is phoning for groceries, which are delivered daily—he will go hunting with the first change in the weather.

BEARING HIS SACK over his shoulder like a burglar, he makes his way down toward the river. In the darkness, each house is fortified by its hard pool of light, and he half expects that his flashlight, spotted at the wood edge by some nosy oldster out of bed to pee, will bring police from all directions, filling the suburban night with whirling red, white, and blue beacons—the Nigger Hunters, as the hotel clerk referred to them, conveying contempt for cops and blacks alike.

In the woods he descends wet shadow paths, his sack catching and twisting in the thorns. At the track edge he peers north and south through a grim mist that hides him entirely from the world, then crosses the railroad to the river.

He lobs the decoys out upon the current, and the wind skids them quickly to the end of their strings, which swing too far inshore. In daybreak light, in choppy water, they in no way resemble three lorn ducks yearning for the companionship of a fourth.

He yanks his blind together, scrunching low as a train sweeps past toward the city. He feels clumsy, out of place, not nearly so well hidden as he had imagined. The upstate passengers, half-dozing in the fetid yellow light, cannot have seen him, though they stare straight at him through the grit-streaked windows. He breaks the light gun, loads two shells, and snaps it to, then sips his cup of coffee, peering outward.

As forecast, the wind is out of the northeast. Pale gulls sail past. But there is no rain, and the mist lifts, and the sun rises from the woods behind, filling the cliff faces across the river with a red-gold light.

The eerie windshine of the first day of a northeaster exposes the decoys for the poor things they are; the unnatural brightness of their anchor lines would flare a wild bird from five gunshots away. His folly is jeered at by clarion jays that cross back and forth among the yellow maples at the wood edge.

BANG

He has whirled and with a quick snap shot extinguished one of the jays, which flutters downward in the river woods like a blue leaf. He sinks back, strangely out of breath. And he is about to break his gun, retreat, slink home—he wants to drink—when there comes a small whispery sound, a small watery rush.

A black duck has landed just beyond the decoys. Struggling to make sense of its silent company, it quacks softly, turning back and forth. It rides the gray wavelets, wheat-colored head held high in wariness.

He has one shell left and no time to reload.

The gentle head switches back and forth, one eye seeking, then the other. In the imminence of the morning sun, in the wild light, the bird's tension holds the earth together.

194

The duck springs from the surface with a downward buffet of the wings. In one jump it is ten feet in the air, drops of water falling, silver-lined wings stretched to the wind that will whirl it out of range.

BANG

The dark wings close. The crumpled thing falls humbly to the surface, scarcely a splash, as the echo caroms from the cliffs across the river.

In the ringing silence, the river morning is resplendent. Time resumes, and the earth breathes again.

The duck floats upside down, head underwater, red legs on the bronze-black feathers twitching.

Not a difficult shot, his father would have said. *The trigger is squeezed when the bird levels off at the top of the jump, for just at that moment it seems almost motionless, held taut by wires*—not *a difficult shot.*

How often in his boyhood he had missed it, turning away so as not to see his father's mouth set at the corners. Then one day he outshot his father, finishing up with a neat double, trying not to grin.

With that second barrel he had overshot his limit. He had known this but could not resist, his father's good opinion had seemed more important. The Assistant Secretary's nod acknowledged the fine shot, but his voice said, *You've always been good at things, Henry. No need to be greedy.* It was no use blustering that he had followed through the double as his father had taught him. His father had no patience with excuses.

Often his mother felt obliged to say, *Your father's standards are so high, you see.*

195

When he tried to ask just what she meant, she cut him off.

She smiled. *Sometimes what I think you lack is a sense of humor.*

He whirls his retrieval rig around his head and lets it go, looping the casting plug out beyond the duck, then tugging it back across the line of drift. On the third try it catches in the tail feathers and turns the bird around before pulling free. The next two tries are rushed, the last falls short.

The current has taken the diminished thing, it is moving more rapidly now, tending offshore.

Alone on the riverbank, peering about him, he takes a deep breath and regrets it, for the breath displaces his exhilaration, drawing into his lungs intuitions of final loneliness and waste and loss. That this black duck of the coasts and rivers should be reduced to a rotting tatter in the tidal flotsam, to be pulled at by the gulls, to be gnawed by rats, is not bearable, he cannot bear it, he veers from this bitter end of things with a grunt of pain. Or is it, he wonders, the waste that he cannot bear?

Something else scares him: he dreads going home alone and empty-handed, to the life still to be lived in the finished cottage. If the hunt supper does not take place, nothing will follow.

Sooner or later, the black duck must enter an eddy and be brought ashore. Hiding the shells and thermos under the driftwood, abandoning the decoys to the river, he hurries down the tracks toward the city, gun across his shoulder.

The bird does not drift nearer, neither does it move out farther. Wind and current hold it in equilibrium, a dull dark thing like charred deadwood in the tidal water. Far ahead, the cliffs of both shores come together at the George Washington Bridge, and beyond the high arch, the sinking skyline of the river cities.

The world is littered with these puppet dictators of ours, protecting our rich businessmen and their filthy ruination of poor countries, making obscene fortunes off the misery of the most miserable people on this earth!

The Assistant Secretary shifted his bones for a better look at his impassive son, as if he had forgotten who he was. He considered him carefully in a long mean silence. *Who do you really work for these days, Henry? What is it that you do, exactly?*

I am the government liaison with the western corporations.

And it's your idea, I'm told, that these corporations pay these governments for the right to dump their toxic wastes in Africa.

When his son was silent, the old man nodded. *I gather they pay you well for what you do.*

Mother says you are obliged to sell the house. I'd like to buy it.

Absolutely not! I'd sooner sell it to Mobutu!

Didn't you warn me once against idealism? The Cold War is not going to be won by the passive intrigues of your day—

Stop that at once! Don't talk as if you had standards of your own—you don't! You're some damn kind of moral dead man! You don't know who the hell you are, and I don't either! You probably should have been an undertaker!

The old man rummaged his newspaper. When his son sat down by him, he drew his dressing gown closer. Stricken, he said, *Forgive me. Perhaps you cannot help what you have become. I asked too much of you, your mother says, I was too*

197

harsh. He paused for a deep breath, then spoke shyly. *I'm sorry, Henry. Please don't come again.*

THE MIST has lifted, the sun rises.

Trudging south, he is overtaken by the heat, the early trains. In his rain parka with the stiff canvas beneath, lugging the gun, his body suffocates. It is his entire body, his whole being, that is growing angry. The trains roar past, they assail him with bad winds, faces stare stupidly. He waves them off, his curses lost in the trains' racketing. His jaw set in an iron rage, he concentrates on each railroad tie, tie after tie.

The dead bird is fifty yards offshore, bound for the sea. In the distance, the silver bridge glints in the mist. Nearer are the cliffs at Spuyten Duyvil, where the tracks turn eastward, following the East River. Once the bird had passed that channel mouth, he could only watch as it drifted down the west shore of Manhattan.

He trots a little. He can already see the rail yard and trestle where the tracks bend away under the cliffs.

5

THERE THEY ARE.

Perched on concrete slabs along the bank, thin dark-skinned figures turn dark heads to see this white man coming with a gun. Though the day is warm, they are wearing purple sweatshirts with sharp, pointed hoods drawn tight, as in some archaic sect in Abyssinia.

They pretend to ignore him, he ignores them, too. "Hey," one says, more or less in greeting. Rock music goes loud then soft again as he moves past paper bags, curled orange peels.

In painted silver, the purple sweatshirts read:

LUMUMBA LIVES

On a drift log lies a silver fish, twenty pounds or more, with lateral black stripes from gills to tail. In the autumn light, the silver scales glint with tints of brass. Should he tell these Africans that this shining New World fish carries cancer-causing poison in its gut?

Beyond the Africans, on the outside of the tracks between rails and river, is a small brick relay station. The wrecked windows are boarded up with plywood, and each plywood panel is marked with a single word scrawled in harsh black:

NAM COKE RUSH

Crouched behind the station, he hides the gun under a board, slips his wallet into a crevice, then his shoulder holster. He fits a shard of brick.

The plaint of a train, from far upriver. The Africans teeter on their slabs, craning to see where he has gone. The sun disappears behind swift clouds.

He strips to his shorts and picks his way across dirtied weeds and rocks, down to the water edge.

Where an eddy has brought brown scud onto the shore lie tarred scrap wood and burnt insulation, women's devices in pink plastic, rusted syringes, a broken chair, a large filth-matted fake-fur toy, a beheaded cat, a spent condom, a half grapefruit.

Ah shit, he says aloud, as if the sound of his own voice might be of comfort. He forces his legs into the flood, flinching in anticipation of glass shards, metal, rusty nails through splintered wood.

199

The hooded figures shout, waving their arms. They yell again, come running down the bank.

His chest is hollowed out, his lungs yawn mortally. He hurls himself outward, gasping as the hard cold strikes his temples, as a soft underwater shape nudges his thigh. In his thrash, he gasps up a half mouthful of the bitter water, losing his breath as he coughs it out, fighting the panic.

Rippling along his ear, the autumn water whispers of cold deeps, green-turning boulders. The river is tugging at his arms, heavy as mercury, entreating him to let go, to sink away. Through the earth's ringing he can hear his arms splash, as the surface ear hears the far whistle of a train, as yells diminish.

Cold iron fills his chest, and desolation. It is over now— this apprehension of the end comes to him simply, as if body and soul were giving up together. The earth is taking him, he is far out on the edge, in the turning current.

The duck floats belly up, head underwater, droplets of Adirondack water pearled on the night blue of its speculum, drifting downriver from the sunny bend, from the blue mountains.

His cold hand is dull as wood on the stiffened duck.

The cold constricts him and his throw is clumsy. The effort of the throw takes too much strength. The duck slides away downstream. He swallows more water, coughs and spits, and overtakes it, rolling onto his back to get a breath.

A rock nudges him. He sees bare trees whirl on the sky. The point-head purple hoods loom up, dark faces break.

"Yo, man! Lookin good, man! You all right?"

From the shallows, he slings the duck onto the shore. He crawls onto the rocks, knocks away a hand.

"Easy, man! We tryin to help!"

"Yay man? What's happenin? How come you jumpin in the river?"

"October, man! *Bad* river, man!"

"Never catch no *nigger* swimmin! Not out there!"

"*No*, man! Niggers *sink*! Any fool know *dat*!"

They yell with laughter.

"Niggers *sink*! Tha's about it!"

"Goodbye cruel world, look like to me!"

"Cruel world!" another hoots, delighted. "Tha's about it!"

His wet underwear is transparent. He feels exposed, caught in the open. Rage grasps him, but he has no strength. He fights for breath.

"Hey man? You hearin me? Next time you need duck meat bad as that, you let me know. Go walkin in the park, toss me some crumbs, noose all you want! Two bucks apiece! Yeah man! Gone give you my card!"

They laugh some more. "Gone give the man his *card,* that nigger say!"

"Like to eat fish? We gone fry fish!"

He gazes from one black man to another, trying to bring the turmoil in his head under control. Four are middle-aged, in old suit trousers and broken street shoes. The fifth might be a son, and wears new running sneakers.

LUMUMBA LIVES

They smile at him. He knows these Africans, he knows how well they feign subservience and admiration, laughing at someone when they have him at their mercy. He gets slowly to his feet.

"Who's Lumumba?" he inquires, playing for time.

"Who Lumumba *is*?"

201

This man looks down, he spreads his lettering with all eight fingers, then looks up at the younger man, who must be twenty.

"My boy Junius our Lumumba man. Who Lumumba, Junius?"

"*Frag!*"

"Who Lumumba, Frag?"

The white man coughs. Wasn't that the problem? That he had not liked Lumumba? Wasn't that it?

Ashamed of his elders, Frag rolls his eyes. Frag is feverish and skinny, wild-eyed, angry. "Have Lumumba on your fuckin shirt, don't know who he *is*?" He glares at the white man, who smiles at him.

"Who he *was*, Lumumba Man. He's dead."

Frag shrieks, "You makin fun? You makin fun with me?"

The white man does a stiff shuffle, almost falling. "Wholumumba, wholumumba, wholumumba, WHO!" He is foot-numb, goosefleshed, shuddering with cold. Nothing seems real to him.

The faces in the purple hoods look mystified. He thinks, Come on, get it over with.

He starts out along the rail bed for the relay station, on the dead city stones and broken glass and metal litter.

At a sharp whistle he turns. Frag pitches the duck underhand, too hard, straight at his gut. He lets it fall.

"Shot it and swam for it, almost got drownded," one man says. "So why you *leavin* it? Ain't got no license?"

He points toward their fishing poles, upriver. They have no license, either. And possession of striped bass, he says, is against the law.

They exchange looks of comic disbelief. One raises both hands. "Whoo!" he says.

"Ol' fish washed up out of the river!"

"Yessir, that fish *all* washed up!"

They hoot, delighted, then frown and mutter when he will not laugh with them.

"Hey, we ain't gone *possess* that fish!"

"No, man! We gone *eat* him! You *invited*!"

When he tells them that their fish is poisoned, they stare back in mock outrage.

"Shit, man! Ain't *niggers* poisoned it!"

He goes on, knowing they will follow. They are after his wallet, and the gun.

"Where's that gun at, Whitey?"

There it is. They have come up fast, they are right behind him.

"None of your business, Blacky," he says, and keeps on going. He feels giddy.

"Blacky" is repeated, bandied about. He hears a whoop, a cry of warning, and he turns again.

An older man with silver grizzle at the temples, dark wet eyes, has his hand on Frag's arm. In Frag's hand is a large rock. The others jabber.

"What's happenin, man? What's up wit' you?"

"Come downriver see if we can help, and you just don't do right."

He resumes walking, paying no attention to the rock. Hauteur, he thinks, will always impress Africans. All the same, he feels confused, and tries to focus. On impulse he admits over his shoulder that he hid the gun, since they know this anyway.

"Scared we steal it, right?" Frag's voice is a near-screech.

203

"Seen niggers hangin around, right?" Frag bounces his big rock off a rail.

He wants to shout "Right!" but restrains himself.

An older voice says, "Easy, Junius, don't excite yourself."

"Frag!"

"Easy, Frag, don't excite yourself. You okay, Frag?"

At the relay station, his clothes are undisturbed. He sees the corner of his wallet in the crevice.

NAM COKE RUSH

He pulls the pants on over his wet underwear, realizes that he does this out of modesty, stops himself, strips. They whoop and whistle. When he reaches for his pants a second time, Frag snaps them from his hand.

"Don't like niggers, right? Scared of 'em, right? We smell it! Oh, we *hate* that honky smell, man!"

His foot is right beside the board, he slides his toe beneath it.

"Mister? Frag excites hisself, okay?"

"Truth!" Frag yells. "Fuckin truth, man! We can take it! Don't like niggers, right?"

"Right," he says, because the timing is so satisfying. He doesn't care whether or not it's true. Five blacks, one white—a clear case of self-defense. He flips the board, stoops quick, brings up the gun.

"Let's have those pants," he says. "I'm tired of this."

The black men back away, form a loose circle neither out of range nor close enough to threaten him. Breathing raggedly, beside himself, Frag stays where he is, as if transfixed by the twin black holes of the gun muzzle.

204   "Don' point that mothafucka, man!" he gasps at last.

"Toss the man his damn pants, Junius! Go ahead, now!"

"Man might do it, Junius! See them eyes?"

"Fuck!" Frag yells, beside himself. "Li'l popgun!"

The father's soft voice is a plea. "Easy, mister, please, what's up wit' you? That boy can't help hisself."

He sees their fear of what they take to be his naked craziness.

At the train whistle, the black men look relieved. Frag jabs his finger, furious and scared. He keeps staring at the gun, he will not back off.

"Toss the man them pants now, Junius."

The train is coming down the track toward the city, loud as a riveting machine, as a machine gun.

"Train comin, man."

But he makes no move to hide himself. He steps farther out onto the tracks. What the engineer must see is a naked white man surrounded and beset by a gang of blacks.

The train blows three shrill whistles, lurches, and begins to slow.

"Junius? Trouble, boy! You got enough!"

"Shit!" the boy snarls. "Ain't us done nothin!"

He slings the pants. The older man grabs him from behind, spins him away. The boy curses in a vicious stream, angling out across the tracks toward the woods on the river slope behind the train, ready to run if anyone on the train starts to descend. He yells, "You ain't done with Frag yet, shithead! Honky mothafuck!"

The train eases to a stop. A hiss of steam. High cirrus clouds come out over the trees, over the river.

"Put them pants on, mister! Folks is *lookin* at you!"

"Back up," he says, lifting the gun. And right now,

205

remembering that both shells in the gun have been expended, he feels a sharp tingle at the temples.

A voice from the train calls, "You all right?" He waves his hand, then lays the gun down and begins to dress.

Sullen and sad, the black men shake their heads. They mutter, but they do not speak, they will not meet the stares from the train windows. They watch him dress, watch him take his wallet from the crevice in the wall. When he straps on the empty shoulder holster, they groan and retreat farther.

The train departs. He starts away, walking upriver.

He wonders now if they meant him any harm, but he takes no chances. Every little while he turns to be sure he is not followed.

The figures stand in silhouette. Three wave and point as the fourth raises the wild duck, bill pointed against the city. They seem to entreat him, but it is too late. What are they calling?

The hurled duck arches on the sky, falls fast, and bounces, coming to rest in the junk along the river.

When he goes back for it, they scatter, abandoning their fish. He puts the gun down, raises both his arms. "Wait a minute!" he calls. "Listen!"

"Get outta here!" they holler back. "Jus' you get *outta* here!"

AT HIS BLIND he retrieves his equipment, leaving the three decoys to the river. With his burlap sack, he starts across the tracks toward the woods. Near the mouth of the old brook, he spins, recoiling from a clip of wind right past his ear.

A purple hood sinks back behind the auto body in the

swamp. He circles the auto, crouching and running, but the rock-thrower has vanished, and the woods are silent.

He hunts quickly through the woods, chasing scared footfalls, then retreats half backward, swinging the gun. Moving slowly so that Frag can tail him without difficulty, he climbs the steep lawn below his father's house. Someone is shouting.

Inside, the cottage seems to enclose him. He listens to the clock tick. The house creaks. He pours himself a whiskey.

No one answers at the real-estate office. To the answering machine he whispers, "This is Henry Harkness. I have a wild duck here, and some wild rice and good wine. I was hoping you and . . ." He doesn't want to say "your wife," but he cannot recall the round-eyed woman's name. He puts the phone down. Somewhere his life took a turn without his knowledge.

The duck drips blood and water from its bill onto the white enamel of the kitchen table.

He slips out the back door and through the trees to the autumn garden. From here he can spot the purple hood coming up along the woods. The running, the game of it, the ambush are exhilarating, but the excitement dies quickly with the whiskey flush and does not return.

He settles down to wait behind the wall.

The light has gone wrong in some way. The sky is darkening in the noon sun, the dusk is waiting in the trees, and nowhere is there any shelter.

The African will come, perhaps at dark. Even now that face is peering from the trees. Neighbors will come to pay respects once it is over.

A police car comes and goes, lights flashing slowly,

humping around the drive on its fat tires. The caretaker rides in the front seat.

No one comes up from the woods, the glinting river. Still he waits there in the autumn garden, cooling his forehead on the night-blue metal, in the haunted sunlight, in the dread of home.

1988

ABOUT THE AUTHOR

PETER MATTHIESSEN was born in New York City in 1927 and had already begun his writing career by the time he graduated from Yale University in 1950. The following year, he was a founder of *The Paris Review*. Besides *At Play in the Fields of the Lord,* which was nominated for the National Book Award, he has published four other novels, including *Far Tortuga.* Mr. Matthiessen's unique career as a naturalist and explorer has resulted in numerous and widely acclaimed books of nonfiction, among them *The Tree Where Man Was Born,* which was nominated for the National Book Award, and *The Snow Leopard,* which won it. His other works of nonfiction include *The Cloud Forest* and *Under the Mountain Wall* (which together received an Award of Merit from the National Institute of Arts and Letters), *The Wind Birds, Blue Meridian, Sand Rivers, In the Spirit of Crazy Horse, Indian Country,* and, most recently, *Men's Lives.* His new novel is *Killing Mister Watson.*